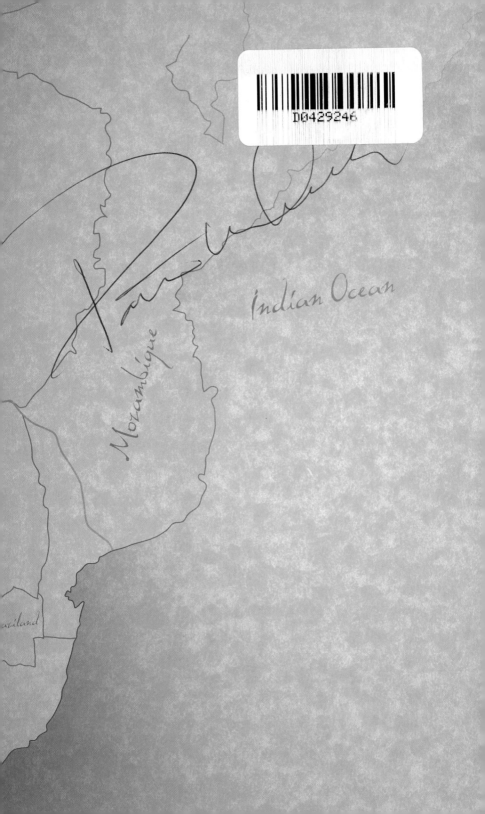

Indian Ocean

Mozambique

Travels with Gannon and Wyatt

Botswana

Travels with Gannon and Wyatt

Botswana

Inspired by the real-life travels of Gannon & Wyatt

*A portion of the proceeds from this book
will go to the Bushmen of the Kalahari*

Copyright © 2009 Claim Stake Publishing

Published by Claim Stake Publishing, LLC

PO Box 1586, Aspen, CO, 81611

www.claimstakeproductions.com

Travels with Gannon and Wyatt: Botswana, 1st ed.

by Patti Wheeler and Keith Hemstreet

ISBN-10: 936284-00-6

ISBN-13: 978-1-936284-00-9

Manufactured by BookMasters

30 Amberwood Parkway, Ashland, OH, 44805

Job#: M7237, March 2010

Graphic design and cover art by Leon Godwin

Photography by Keith Hemstreet, Wyatt Wheeler,

Patti Wheeler, and Gannon Wheeler

Book edited by Cindy Hirschfeld

Website Design by Kissane Viola Design

For more info visit:

www.travelswithgannonandwyatt.com

Acknowledgments

We would like to thank Tom, our dad, for his support and encouragement, Ms. Heidi for keeping watch over the children during our journey, and Doug and Nancy Van Howd for introducing us to the magic of Africa. Without you, this book would not be possible.

"*Travel is fatal to prejudice, bigotry,
and narrow-mindedness.*"

–Mark Twain

"*Do not follow where the path may lead. Go instead
where there is no path and leave a trail.*"

–Ralph Waldo Emerson

Youth Exploration Society Banquet
The Mayflower Hotel
Washington, D.C.

*"What the world needs now, more than ever, are leaders
in the youth community. Leaders who will inspire
others to do their part to protect the environment.
Leaders who will fight to save the last great
wildernesses. Leaders who will volunteer their time
to help those who are less fortunate. If young people
become passionate about the well being of our planet–its
people, its wildlife, its environment–a bright future will
be ensured for generations to come. Here today, we
have two such young men...."*

> –Dr. Bernard Fuller
> *An excerpt from his speech
> announcing the winners of the
> Livingstone Prize*

Table of Contents

Part I

Part II

Part III

Part IV

English/Setswana:
Translation of Common Phrases

Hello, Sir / Madam - *Dumela, rra/mma*
How are you? - *O kae?*
I am fine - *Ke teng*
What is your name? - *Leina la gago ke mang?*
My name is - *Leina la me ke*
Where are you from? - *O tswakae?*
Please - *Tswee-tswee*
Thank you, Sir / Madam - *Ke a leboga, rra/mma*
I'm hungry - *Ke tshwerwe ke tlala*
I'm thirsty - *Ke tshwerwe ke lenyora*
I like - *Ke rata*
I don't like - *Ga ke rate*
Where is the hospital? - *Kokelwana e ko kae?*
I need help, please - *Ke kopa thuso, tswee-tswee*
May I help you? - *A nka go thusa?*
Goodbye - *Tsamaya sentle*

Part I:

Who we are and why we write books

Wyatt: "It's in our blood."

My brother and I are travelers. We did not come by this on our own, though I would like to think we would have if given the chance. The truth is, we owe it all to our parents. You see, my mom grew up in a podunk town in north Florida that you've probably never heard of. It's so small it's not even on most maps. When she was a little girl she'd lie on her back in the itchy Florida crabgrass and watch the planes fly overhead. She always wished she was on one of them. It didn't matter where they were going, she said, as long as it was somewhere new and exciting.

This fascination with travel really got into her blood. Not long after she turned seventeen she walked to the bus station and spent all her savings on a ticket to the city to interview for a job with an airline. You had to be at least eighteen years old to work for the airline, so what did my mom do? She lied, of course, and told them she was eighteen. The airline called my grandma, who also lied about my mom's age so that she could get the job. Believe it or not, they hired her on the spot. Now, I'm not one to promote dishonesty, but I have to say, I sure am thankful my mom and grandma didn't have a problem with it. If it weren't for their little white lie, you probably wouldn't be reading this book right now.

Here's the thing—when you work for an airline, your entire family gets to fly all over the world for free. Now don't go telling everyone about this free flying business or all sorts of parents will go running to the airlines looking for jobs and that will just create a huge headache for everyone involved. Not to mention the fact that having thousands of parents show up looking for jobs might make the airlines reconsider this free flying thing altogether. If we were no longer allowed to fly for free, we'd end up stuck in the same place every day, and that would get awfully boring. You know what, just forget I ever mentioned it, okay?

Good, now where was I? Oh, that's right. I was telling you about my parents. Well, you know about my mom, so I guess I'll tell you a little bit about my dad. He's an artist and enjoys exploring all of the beautiful places you come across when traveling. I guess that's what artists do. They look for beauty in the world and then try to create their own interpretation of it in paintings, sculptures, books or whatever. When something catches my dad's eye, he will flip open his sketch pad and make a drawing. Later he'll use his drawings to paint a canvas, or sometimes he'll even make a sculpture, like the one he made of the tiger that chased us in India. But that's another story for another time.

I really don't have much more to say about my parents. I love them and all, but they're my parents–and parents aren't exactly the most interesting topic of conversation. Besides, the point of this book is not to tell the life story of my parents. If I did that I'd bore you to tears, and you'd probably run down to the bookstore and demand your money back. The point of this book is to tell you about an awesome adventure my brother and I had in the African bush.

Official seal of the Youth Exploration Society
- Wyatt

After we got back from our safari, the Youth Exploration Society gave us the prestigious Livingstone Prize, named after Dr. David Livingstone, a Scottish missionary who spent much of his life exploring Africa. We went to Washington, D.C., to accept the award and gave a presentation with video and photographs of our adventure. Public speaking is nerve-wracking, but here's a trick. Picture the audience in their underwear. I'm serious. Your nerves will vanish. Try it sometime. It works.

After the award ceremony, we were approached by Dr. Bernard Fuller, professor of environmental science at Georgetown University. Dr. Fuller told us he had traveled the world and written several books on exploration, foreign cultures, wildlife and the environment and thought we might be interested in doing the same.

Although the idea of becoming an author was exciting, I knew that writing a book would be a huge undertaking. However, my brother and I had each kept journals during our travels (it was required as part of our home schooling) and knew that we wouldn't have to write these books from scratch, which would probably take the rest of our lives, so we agreed.

Dr. Fuller loved our tales of adventure. Over the years, we've been stalked by predators and hunted by poachers, rafted raging rivers, trekked across some of the world's highest mountain ranges, explored the Arctic and Antarctic, sailed the South Seas, investigated the mysteries of ancient ruins, hiked through jungles, and been stranded on an uninhabited island, among other things.

Anyhow, Dr. Fuller told us that our adventures were the type of things people like to read about. I prefer reading about scientific stuff, but if my journals encourage even one person to explore some place they've never been, then I guess this whole book project is worth it. You've probably never heard this from any of your teachers before, but, in my opinion, exploration is the best way to acquire knowledge. Sure, books are wonderful and all, but if you really want to learn about a place, you need to see it with your own eyes.

Gannon: "The world is my classroom."

I'm guessing my brother has already bored you with specific details of this, that and the other thing. Sometimes he'll get to yapping about the digestive system of a giraffe or the highest recorded temperature in the Kalahari Desert or the latitude and longitude of the Galapagos Islands, and my head will start to spin. He thinks he's Charles Darwin reincarnated or something. I guess some people get into all that stuff, but not me. Science bores me. I don't care how many hours a day an elephant spends eating grass or how to navigate through the bush using the stars, so I don't write about that stuff.

What you'll find in my journal are the personal things I've experienced while traveling. In short, the things that left a lasting impression. To me, that's what matters most. I'm not trying to be all profound or anything. But if you get wrapped up in the details of things, like my obsessive-compulsive brother, well, sometimes you miss what's really important. For example, a smile from an Eskimo child in an Arctic village or the glow in a lion's eyes at sundown.

Now, of course, that's just my opinion. Everyone sees things differently. That's why if you sent ten people on the same trip, you'd probably hear ten different stories when they got back. Everyone has different interests and different opinions about things. My brother and I are no different.

In addition to keeping my daily journal during our travels, I also carry a video camera. It's a high-definition camera, just like the pros use, and it comes with me everywhere I go. I bought it secondhand from a filmmaker in London, England, cleaned it up, bought a new battery and, sure enough, it's worked like a charm ever since. Other than traveling and the people I meet along the way, I'd say film is my biggest passion. I like to think of myself as an auteur. That's someone who makes movies. Maybe some day National Geographic will hire me, and I will send them amazing footage from every continent, and then I'll be a "world-famous" auteur. I mean, really, can you think of a career cooler than traveling around the world making movies?

Before we get into our story, I've been asked to describe my family so you can understand where we come from, why we travel, etc. I know my brother has done this, too, so I'll be brief.

If I could describe our family in one word, I'd use the word "nomadic." Nomadic means never settling in one place. Sure, we have a home like most everyone else. It's in the United States, in the mountains of Colorado to be more specific. But we travel so much, we're rarely there. I don't even like calling it home so much. I like to think the entire world is my home, though that goes against what most people have been taught all their lives. A home, most of us think, is where we have our stuff–our bed and clothes and books and games–but I don't really agree. My home is wherever I happen to go to bed that night, be it a hotel in Hong Kong or a sailboat off the coast of Fiji.

My brother and I have been home schooled most of our lives. Lucky for us, my mother is an amazing teacher. So is my dad, for that matter. A typical school day goes like this:

In the morning we'll do some math and stuff. Then for the rest of the day, we go exploring.

Before dinner, we'll spend some time writing in our journals. Finally, we'll sit around the fire and read aloud from our favorite books or tell stories of great explorers of the past, like Sacagawea, the Native American woman who helped guide Lewis and Clark across North America, or Sir Edmund Hillary, who with Tenzing Norgay was the first man to climb Mount Everest, the world's tallest mountain. (FYI–My brother just told me that Everest stands exactly 29,035 feet above sea level. For some reason, he has this fact committed to memory.)

You might be wondering whether I miss being in a real school. Well, I have an answer. Undeniably, undoubtedly, emphatically and without hesitation, "no." I like my classroom overlooking a lagoon in Bora Bora, thank you very much, or on the deck of a log cabin in Alaska, where a moose might just walk up and say hello. You can have your concrete walls and blackboards. I don't care for them. I like being nomadic.

Okay, let's not waste any more time on me. You bought this book to read a story, so a story we'll give you–and a pretty amazing one at that. Ever since we'd returned from our adventure in the Great Bear Rainforest, where we went in search of the mythical "Spirit Bear," we had been itching to begin another journey. So that night after dinner, we each wrote down our destination of choice on small pieces of paper. My mom gathered our votes and read them aloud. Amazingly, we'd all chosen the same place: Africa!

Part II:

Journey to the Dark Continent

Gannon
Journal Entry Date: August 21
Location: Flight 712, Seat 42B, somewhere over the Atlantic Ocean

It's a seventeen-hour flight from Washington, D.C., to Johannesburg, South Africa, where we'll have a short layover before flying to Maun, Botswana. We're fourteen hours into the flight and still somewhere over the Atlantic Ocean, but nearing the southwestern coast of Africa. The sun is coming up, painting the sky in all the colors of the rainbow. I must say, there are few things as spectacular as a sunrise from 38,000 feet.

During the night I only slept three or four hours, but I feel surprisingly alert. I'm sure it has something to do with our destination. In all of our travels, I don't think I've ever been so excited!

When I told my friends we were going to Africa, almost everyone asked why. It made me wonder if my friends would ever venture beyond their own backyards. I mean, who asks "why" about the chance to travel? I say, "Why not?" Why not expand your horizons? Why not learn about new cultures? Why not see what there is beyond your home turf?

Looking out my window, I've noticed that we are over land. The Country of Namibia is directly below us. The early morning sun lights the desert. Other than long dirt roads that disappear into the haze, there are no signs of anything man made. No cities, no towns. Just land, as far as the eye can see.

Wyatt
Journal Entry Date: August 21
Location: Maun, Botswana
Time: 12:24 PM
Temperature: 21 Celsius, 74 Fahrenheit
Skies: Clear
Wind: Calm

Just before 11 AM, we landed in Maun, a dusty town of about 100,000 people in north-central Botswana. I am sitting on the steps outside the airport. A man just walked up and asked if I wanted to buy any bananas. I looked into the man's bag, thinking that a banana might actually hit the spot and provide a good dose of potassium to help keep my muscles working properly, but the bananas were all too ripe and bruised. Maybe that's the way they like to eat them here, but there wasn't one in the bunch that looked appetizing to me. Politely, I said, "No, thank you" and moved on.

We are waiting for a connecting flight to our camp in the Kalahari Desert, which is about an hour away. We'll be flying on a small plane. That would scare some people, but I love small planes. When you're in a small plane you really get the sensation of flying, of moving through the sky from one point to another. Whereas in a jumbo jet, you more or less feel like you're in a giant movie theater or something. When we landed in Maun I took a look in the hangar and saw a few Caravans, which seat eleven or twelve people, and even a couple Cessna 206s, which only seat six, including the pilot. Both are single-engine planes and from what I've been told, very reliable.

The purpose of our trip is to go on safari. We'll start out by exploring the Kalahari Desert, a stretch of dunes and salt pans, which covers over 100,000 square miles in Botswana, Namibia and South Africa. We'll live in tents near a Bushmen village and attempt to track the great white rhino.

FACT: Anthropologists believe the Bushmen, or San people, have lived in the Kalahari Desert for over 30,000 years.

After a week in the Kalahari, we will fly to the Okavango Delta, a system of inland waterways fed by the Cubango River. The Cubango is filled each year by monsoon rains that fall in Angola's highlands to the north. The floods from these rains provide lots of water to the delta; and where there is water, there is wildlife.

FACT: The size of the delta is always changing. During the high season, the delta can swell to over 6,000 square miles. When the water levels recede during the dry season, the size of the delta shrinks to under 3,500 square miles. Even during the dry season, the Okavango Delta is said to be one of the largest inland water systems in the world.

I have to tell you, I've been so excited about this trip that I've hardly been able to sleep for a week. Having the chance to go into the African bush and observe the wildlife in an environment that has hardly changed in thousands of years, well, that's every budding scientist's dream.

And now, just a short thirty hours after leaving Denver, Colorado, I am here! It's really amazing to think that just yesterday I was having breakfast in North America, and now I'm in Africa. It's like my mom always says, "Any place in the world, no matter how far, is just a few flights away."

As I write this, I'm watching my brother walk aimlessly down the sidewalk, stopping to talk to random people. It's anybody's guess what he's asking these people. With his blond hair and blue eyes, the kid sticks out like a sore thumb. But that doesn't seem to faze him. I have to admit, I don't know anyone else who can strike up conversations with total strangers like my brother does. He's a real people person.

Gannon
Journal Entry Date: Tuesday (I think)

After we got to Maun, we had some time before we flew to camp, so I did what I normally do in a new place. I walked around and talked to the locals.

TRAVELER'S NOTE: When you arrive in a new place, it's not always a good idea to walk around and talk to people on your own. Some places, to be honest, are downright danger-ous, and you could end up in a lot of trouble if you venture into the streets by yourself. It's always smart to research your destination be-fore you travel. If you take the time to educate yourself, you will know which destinations are safe to explore and which ones are not.

I like to say hello to the people who live there. Whenever I do this, I try to say something in the native language. In my opinion, doing so shows that you respect the local culture. But different people react differently to a perfect stranger walking up to say hello. For example, when I was in Russia, not many people said hello back. They usually just walked by, looking at me like I was a little bit crazy. Apparently, it's not a Russian custom to greet strangers on the street. Come to think of it, people acted the same way in New York City. So maybe it's a big city thing, not just a Russian thing. But in my opinion, friendliness can be understood anywhere, by anyone. Whether people say hello back or not, I'm pretty confident that they will remember me at some point and say, "You know, that boy who said hello to me was very friendly. If everyone were so friendly, the world would be a better place." At least, that's my hope.

Exploring Maun was lots of fun. I came across an old man seated behind a small booth on the side of the street. I greeted him using some Setswana words that I'd studied on the plane. Setswana, other than English, is the official language of Botswana.

"Hallo," I said to the man. "*Leina la ka ke,* Gannon. *Ketswako* United States. *O bua Sekhowa?*"

Translation to English: "Hello. My name is

Gannon. I'm from the United States. Do you speak English?"

It turned out the man did speak English. He was nice enough to offer me a chair, and we started talking. He told me that he was born in Maun and had lived there his whole life. He wasn't born in a hospital like me. He was born in a hut that his father had built from mud, sticks and tree branches. The floor of the hut was mostly dirt, but in one area there was a small rug. His mother delivered him right on the rug. His brother and sister were born on the rug, too. Can you imagine that?

The man talked about how he'd seen Maun grow from a tiny village of mud huts to a sprawling town with concrete office buildings, restaurants and shops. He said the town had grown because safaris were attracting more and more visitors every year.

The man spent most days at his booth selling wooden sculptures that he and his wife carve with their own hands. This man had never gone to school to learn how to carve wood and neither had his wife. They taught themselves how to do it through trial and error. But judging by the quality of their artwork, I would have guessed that they had been taught at a school for sculptors in Paris or Rome.

I bought a small wooden elephant for my cousin Bliss. She's five years old and loves big animals, especially elephants. I didn't have any Botswanan money, but the man said he would gladly accept U.S. dollars. He charged me $2. I don't know much about valuing art, but $2 seemed like an amazing deal for this sculpture. I thanked the man the best I could in Setswana: "*Ke a leboga.*" He smiled. Partly for my business and partly, I bet, because I butchered his language.

As I walked back to the airport, I noticed a rusty old jeep on the side of the road. As I came closer, I saw a sinister-looking man putting several rifles in the back. You know how there are certain people who bring about an uneasy feeling in the pit of your stomach? Well, this guy was one of those people. He wore a beat-up safari hat, and there was a patch over his left eye. But it wasn't so much the eye patch that gave me the creeps. What really creeped me out was the man's good eye. It was completely black, like some kind of marble. I'm not kidding–there was no color whatsoever.

As I passed the jeep, the man turned and glared at me with his dark eye. It sent a chill down my spine. I turned away and double-timed it back to the airport, hoping that I'd never see this man again as long as I lived.

Wyatt
Journal Entry Date: August 21
Location: Kalahari Desert, Botswana
Time: 7:34 PM
Temperature: 18 Celsius, 68 Fahrenheit
Skies: Clear
Wind: Calm

The Cessna 206 that flew us to the Kalahari
- Wyatt

We flew to camp in a Cessna 206, like I had hoped. You would think that my mom, who has worked for the airlines for so many years, would be comfortable in any plane, but she was as scared as a little kid on a rickety old rollercoaster.

When she first saw the plane, her eyes got really wide. "Is this our plane?" she asked. "Please tell me this is not our plane." When she found out it was, in fact, our plane, she turned white as a ghost.

Soon after the pilot started the engine, my mom began sniffing the air like a dog does when it's looking for food. "Does anyone smell smoke?" she said. "I smell smoke. Something is burning!"

No one else smelled smoke. I think it was all in her imagination.

As the plane lifted off, it was bounced around by a stiff wind. I really thought my mom might faint. My dad laughed out loud at the sight of my mom, who had her eyes closed and a white-knuckle grip on the armrests. Maybe it was the pilot, who looked like he was barely eighteen years old, or maybe it was the toy-like size of the plane, or maybe it was a fear that flight regulations in Botswana aren't as strict as they are in other parts of the world. Whatever it was, my mom was terrified.

With four passengers plus baggage, the Cessna 206 was literally packed from floor to ceiling, but somehow we managed to all fit. After I lost to Gannon in a game of rock-paper-scissors, he got to sit in the co-pilot seat. I was totally bummed because sitting up front makes you feel like you're actually flying the plane. But even sitting in back with my camera pack on my lap, I enjoyed the flight. According to the altimeter, we were cruising between 4,900 and 5,000 feet above sea level. We were still low enough, though, to get a great view of the Kalahari Desert.

Gannon in the co-pilot seat - Wyatt

During the flight, we passed over several brush fires; at times the air was so hazy you couldn't even see the ground. The pilot told us that fires often start when lightning strikes the dry brush, but that lately poachers have been starting fires in order to trap animals and make it easier to hunt them.

Poachers are people who illegally hunt animals for their valuable skins, furs, ivory tusks, horns, etc. Poachers pose a great threat to the wildlife, since the more animals they kill, the more money they make. I hope the fires we saw were started by lightning. I love new experiences, but a run-in with a poacher is an experience I could do without.

We landed on a small dirt and potholed airstrip in the western Kalahari. From the airstrip we were driven over bumpy dirt roads, kicking up huge clouds of dust as we weaved our way through the desert brush. Yellow flowers budded on thorny acacia bushes. The leaves of umbrella trees made circles of shade on the sand. We even saw a kudu peek its head out from behind a shrub.

As we neared the camp, the sun began to go down. It turned bright red, like a lollipop, and painted the sky in neon oranges and purples. I've seen some beautiful sunsets in my day, but a sunset in the Kalahari Desert tops them all.

At Edo's Camp, a cluster of tents that would be our home for the next week, we were greeted by our guide, Chocs, and his daughter, Jubjub. A native of Botswana, Chocs was tall and strong, with the most perfect white teeth I'd ever seen. Chocs had gone to a university in England and earned a degree in environmental science and zoology. When he got back to Botswana, he'd started a safari business—a perfect choice given his education and love of wildlife.

Jubjub was born and raised in the bush. Because her father's work kept them traveling back and forth between the Kalahari and the Okavango Delta, Jubjub was home schooled just like us. Her mother, who Chocs had met when he was a child, managed the family's safari business.

Jubjub seemed very confident and mature, which I guess is inevitable when you grow up in an environment as wild as this. When I said that I liked her name, she told me that Jubjub means "savior."

We all gathered around the fire pit underneath a sprawling camel thorn tree. A dozen or so wildebeest drank from the watering hole, along with a group of waterbuck and a big male kudu. As the last light faded, and the first stars appeared in the desert sky, the air turned cool.

"I'd like to welcome you all to Botswana and the great Kalahari Desert," Chocs said with a big smile. "There are only a handful of places left in the world where you can enjoy nature in its pristine state. The Kalahari Desert and Okavango Delta are two such places. While in Botswana, you will encounter all of the Big Five. Does anyone know what animals make up the Big Five?"

Gannon raised his hand, and Chocs pointed to him.

"Lions, elephants, leopards, cape buffalo, and...uh...the hippo?"

"Close," Chocs said. "You were correct with the exception of the hippo. It's the rhino, not the hippo that is part of the Big Five. Speaking of rhinos, have a look."

Chocs pointed to the far end of the watering hole. A large white rhino was coming out of the brush. It walked slowly to the edge of the pond, lowered its head and took a drink.

FACT: *Next to the elephant, the white rhino is the largest land-bound mammal on Earth.*

"What a beautiful animal," my father said. "They are so prehistoric. I can't wait to get to work."

My father's job while we're in Botswana is to paint and photograph the white rhino. When we return home he's going to create a life-size sculpture of this rare animal for an art collector in Santa Fe, New Mexico.

Jubjub walked down from the kitchen. "Excuse me," she said. "The wildebeest stew is ready."

Was she serious? Wildebeest stew? Just the sound of it made my stomach turn. Then again, I suppose you'll never know whether or not you'll like something until you try it. As I've heard people say, "When in Rome, do as the Romans do."

"If we can all follow Jubjub to the dining tent," Chocs said, "we've prepared a wonderful African meal for you. I hope you are all ready for an adventure, because an adventure is what we have in store."

Gannon
Time: Early morning

Last night, after our meal of wildebeest stew (it was okay, but not my favorite), I walked back to our tent under a million stars and fell asleep before my head hit the pillow. I was so tired I don't think I would have woken up if a rhino had walked up and licked my face.

It is still winter here in the southern hemisphere. Most people don't think of Africa as being cold, especially when you're talking about the desert. But let me tell you, it gets really, really cold here. So cold, in fact, that Chocs gave us each a hot water bottle to keep under our blankets during the night. This morning I am dressed in long pants, a heavy fleece and a winter jacket, but despite all these clothes, I can't stop shivering as I write. Wyatt's thermometer reads 37 degrees Fahrenheit.

Today Chocs and Jubjub are taking us to a Bushmen village. Traditionally, the Bushmen are hunter-gatherers, which means they hunt and gather food from the land. They've been living this way for tens of thousands of years, but as people buy more and more land around them, the areas where they can hunt get smaller. As a result, most Bushmen have given up hunting and become farmers in order to provide enough food for their families.

The Bushmen way of life is truly fascinating.
I can hardly wait to meet them!

Wyatt
Journal Entry Date: August 22
Location: Kalahari Desert, Botswana
Time: 11:22 AM
Temperature: 14 Celsius, 60 Fahrenheit
Skies: Clear

When Chocs warned us that we had an adventure in store, I doubt he had what happened this morning in mind.

On our way to the Bushmen village, my mom spotted something moving through the acacia trees about fifty yards from the road.

"Stop the jeep!" she yelled, pointing. "I just saw something! And it was big!"

Chocs stopped the jeep and looked through his binoculars. In the distance, he spotted a family of white rhinos casually walking through the bushes.

"A male, a female and two babies," he said. "And they're coming this way. I'm going to turn off the jeep so we don't frighten them."

Jubjub took the binoculars from her father

and looked at the rhinos.

"That's the pregnant mother we saw last month," she said. "She had her babies. They can't be more than a few weeks old."

The jeep didn't have a roof, so we all stood up for a better look. Sure enough, a family of rhinos was coming right toward us. When they came within a hundred feet or so, they stopped, as if they had suddenly sensed that we were near.

"Rhinos have very poor eyesight," Chocs whispered. "But they definitely know we're here."

White rhinos aren't actually white; they're gray, with two horns on the bridge of their snout. The horn closest to their nostrils is about three times the size of the other horn. Their bodies are so massive it seems impossible that their small,

The female rhino staring at us from a safe distance, or so I thought - Wyatt

stubby legs could carry them. Their eyes are like black pinballs, and their ears are twisted like conch shells. In my personal opinion, there is no animal on Earth that looks more like a dinosaur than the rhino.

The rhino family stood very still for awhile, as if they were confused about what to do next. Watching them in awe, I had a false sense of security, like I was watching them from behind a high cement wall at the zoo. But that sense of security vanished the instant one of the babies started trotting our way.

Chocs immediately sprang to his feet, clapping his hands and yelling in an attempt to make the baby turn in a different direction. But the baby continued, jogging right up to the jeep like a puppy looking for a playmate. The second baby followed close behind.

"No!" Chocs yelled. "Go back! Go!"

"Turn around!" Jubjub yelled. "Go back to your mother and father!"

The male and female rhinos were getting angry, jerking their heads around and huffing loudly. When one of the babies disappeared behind the jeep, the female rhino charged.

Chocs dropped into the driver's seat and tried to start the jeep, but the engine sputtered and stalled.

"Everyone hold on tight!" Chocs yelled.

I put my camera down and grabbed onto the roll bar. The ground rumbled, and we all braced for impact, as this giant of the Kalahari thundered toward us. Right up to the last second, I doubted the rhino would actually ram the jeep, assuming she somehow understood that doing so would hurt her more than it hurt the vehicle. Boy, was I wrong.

With a deafening sound, like two cars colliding at high speed, the rhino slammed into the jeep. The vehicle tilted and almost rolled over on its side. My mom lost her grip and fell out the back, landing hard on the ground.

"Mom!" Gannon yelled. He reached out to help her back into the jeep, but the female rhino cut her off before she could climb inside. My mom backed up facing the rhino, her eyes wide with fear. The rhino glared at her and lifted its sharp horn in quick jerks, as if she was warning my mom that she wasn't afraid to use it. My dad jumped out of the jeep and ran to my mom. The male rhino soon joined the attack, swiping hard at the jeep with the side of his head while he circled around us. This constant ramming of the jeep startled the babies, and eventually they ran off into the bushes. The male rhino quickly followed. But the female stood her ground, facing off with my mom and dad. She looked like she was ready to charge at any moment.

Chocs stepped from the jeep and moved slowly toward my parents.

"Everyone talk loudly now!" he said. "Should the rhino charge, run behind that tree to your left! Do you see it?"

"Yes," my mom said, her voice shaking. "I see it."

"Okay, good!" Chocs said. "Now let's everyone continue to talk loudly!"

Everyone followed his instructions.

"We're all talking loudly to the rhinos!" Jubjub said.

"Yes, we're all talking loudly!" my dad echoed.

"Talk loudly, Wyatt!" Gannon said.

Everything was happening so fast, I hadn't realized that I was just standing there silent as a mouse.

"Okay, Gannon! I'm talking loudly now! Talking loudly to the rhinos!"

All of the voices seemed to startle the rhino. She took a few steps back and looked around frantically, as if trying to spot her family.

"That's good!" Chocs continued. "She's moving back! Everyone continue to talk loudly!"

"We're talking loudly!" I said. "Talking loudly! Talking loudly!"

It felt awkward, all of us talking loudly to a

rhino, but it worked. The female rhino eventually turned and ran off, disappearing into the bushes behind a billowing cloud of dust.

My mother was so shaken she could hardly speak. Her hands were trembling like leaves in the wind. Chocs and my dad helped her back into the truck. Once she was safely inside, Gannon and I hugged and kissed her as if we hadn't seen her in years. She'd just cheated death–and it would have been a gruesome one. We knew it, and we were thankful beyond words that she had survived.

"Have you ever had a scare like that?" my dad asked Chocs.

"Not in all my years in Africa," he said.

"Do you ever carry a rifle?"

"In the past, we have not. At least, not in the Kalahari. But after today, I may change that policy."

Chocs went on to explain that the rhinos aggressive behavior was due to their concern about the safety of their newborn babies. A baby rhino's eyesight is even worse than an adult's, so they couldn't see us well enough to know to stay away. The parents, however, knew that their babies might be in danger, and that's why they attacked.

Despite the scare, my mom somehow managed to keep her sense of humor.

"I know I'm the one who asked to stop," she

said, "but next time we see a rhino, I vote we keep driving."

Everyone laughed, which helped calm our nerves just a little.

"I second that vote," said Jubjub.

"Agreed," Chocs said. "No more stopping for rhinos."

Chocs asked my mom if she wanted to return to camp for a rest, but she insisted we continue the day as planned. Chocs then jumped into the driver's seat and turned the ignition. Much to our surprise, the jeep started.

"I can't believe it still works after taking such a beating," my dad said.

"These jeeps are rhino proof," Chocs said with a smile.

I rested my head against the back of the seat and closed my eyes. We were safe. After such a terrible scare, that's a good feeling. But how long would it last? As the desert sun warmed my face, I considered just how much I had underestimated the risk you take when exploring the wilds of Africa. No matter how much you study animal behavior, you never really know what they are going to do. One predator might pay no attention to you. Another might tear you apart. As my mom later said, "A safari is safe...until it isn't."

Gannon
Date: August 22
Time: Evening

I've never received a welcome like the one we received today at the Bushmen village. When we arrived, dozens of children ran up to the jeep, cheering wildly. As soon as I got out of the vehicle, they surrounded me, tugging enthusiastically at my arms and legs. One of the kids even jumped on my back and got a piggyback ride into the village. I felt like a celebrity being mobbed by a group of crazed fans.

In the village, the kids scattered, and we were greeted by the elders. They nodded and bowed slightly, and we all shook hands. This particular tribe has about eighty people, and about thirty of them are children. Some of the kids, despite the

Our new friends, the Naru Bushmen - Gannon

cool morning air, were only wearing loincloths. Others were wrapped in homemade blankets with colorful patterns. Most of them, however, had on random collections of hand-me-downs that had been donated by previous visitors. I recognized the brands on several shirts and saw sweaters and other articles of clothing with the logos of different sports teams, including a New York Yankees baseball cap.

An elder male, his face creased with deep lines, gestured to us, sweeping his hand across the village. It was a welcome invitation, Chocs said, for us to tour the village.

In the village there were about ten mud huts, a small chicken coop, a fenced area with a few goats and a courtyard where women were making various crafts that they would sell to visitors.

As we walked through the courtyard, the children surrounded us again and started singing and dancing.

Unfortunately, I don't speak the Bushmen's language, which is made up of sounds and clicks. But then, not many people can. The language is strictly verbal, meaning there is no written version that you can study. But we were able to overcome the language barrier thanks to Chocs and Jubjub, who over the years had spent enough time with the Bushmen to be able to translate their language into English.

However, when I asked Jubjub to translate a song the kids were singing, she said this particular song didn't contain actual words, only sounds from a song ancestors had been singing since before a Bushmen language existed. The melody was incredible!

My mom was so taken by the children in the village that she volunteered to help them construct a new, bigger school hut so that more children could attend. The Bushmen children are taught English, among other things, so that one day they will be able to negotiate for the tribe when dealing with landowners and the government of Botswana.

Given that the Bushmen have lived the same way for tens of thousands of years, it is unfortunate that they are now having to adapt to our way of life.

A traditional Bushmen hut - Gannon

As Jubjub said, "The Bushmen's traditional way of life is under threat. Sadly, it's a dying culture."

Wyatt
Journal Entry Date: August 22
Location: Kalahari Desert, Botswana
Time: 6:35 PM
Temperature: 17 Celsius, 66 Fahrenheit
Skies: Clear
Wind: Calm

After we toured the Bushmen village, an elder woman led us into the Kalahari bush with some of the children to show us how they gather food and water. We walked slowly, stepping cautiously over the dusty, dry land. I wasn't sure what the Bushmen were looking for, but I was keeping a sharp eye out for two things: 1) rhinos and 2) black mambas, one of the most poisonous snakes on Earth.

About a half hour into the trek, the elder woman bent over and picked up a brown twig about four inches long. She held it up and called to her children. They all gathered around and began digging in the spot where she had found the twig.

"When they find this particular twig,"

Jubjub explained, "they know that there is water underneath."

How she spotted that twig, I can't imagine. To me, it looked just like every other twig in the Kalahari, but she knew that because this twig was a slightly lighter shade than the others, it meant there was water underneath. I watched as they dug, expecting them to uncover a natural spring. But after digging a two-foot hole, there was still no water in sight. Instead, they removed a round gourd the size of a basketball. They then took a long stick and began rubbing it over the gourd's surface, creating a pulp that they piled up in the dirt. Once they had a handful of pulp, they packed it into a ball, held it over their mouths and squeezed. Sure enough, water dripped from the pulp. Each handful of pulp produced about an ounce or two of water.

It amazed me, the work that went into getting a single sip of water. I felt guilty about having two liters of bottled water in my backpack. Watching the Bushmen drink from the shaved gourd, it made me sick to think of how much water most of us waste every day. We take long showers, leave the faucet running and dump out the rest of a glass of water when we're no longer thirsty. Truth is, we take water for granted. I swore to myself then and there that I'd never again waste another drop of water.

The elder women who led us through the Kalahari - Wyatt

Gannon
Time: Afternoon

We all tried a handful of pulp. The water that came out of it was milky and kind of bitter.

Afterward, we continued the gathering expedition and found several potatoes, a second gourd and a handful of small sticks that the Bushmen use to clean their teeth.

Once the elder woman was satisfied, she plopped down in the sand, rolled a cigarette and smoked. Out of respect, we all sat around and waited patiently until she finished. The tobacco, Chocs said, was a gift from previous visitors. I could think of a much better gift for the Bushmen than cigarettes, but I kept my mouth shut.

Wyatt
Journal Entry Date: August 23
Location: Kalahari Desert, Botswana
Time: 5:53 AM
Temperature: 4 Celsius, 40 Fahrenheit
Skies: Clear
Wind: Calm

It's not even light yet, but my father is already up and preparing for a day of photographing the white rhinos. In spite of our frightening encounter yesterday, he can't wait to get up close and personal with the beasts. He's also set up an easel near the watering hole, so that he can make a painting when the rhinos come to drink in the evening.

My mom, obviously wanting nothing to do with rhinos, is going to go back to the Bushmen village to begin building the school hut.

I am going to join Chocs and my dad on their rhino expedition. Gannon is going back to the Bushmen village with Jubjub and mom. It was tough for me to decide what I wanted to do today, as both are unique adventures, not to mention tremendous learning experiences, so I decided to divide my time down the middle. Today I'll go in search of the rhinos; tomorrow I'll go to the Bushmen village.

Gannon
Date: August 23
Time: Morning, just after breakfast

When I arrived at the dining tent for breakfast, I had the pleasure of meeting Tcori (Te-cor-ee), another member of the Bushmen tribe. The son of the elder I met the day before, Tcori was skinny and no more than five and a half feet tall. He had just returned from an expedition in the Okavango Delta.

Like his father's, Tcori's face was weathered from exposure to the harsh African sun. It was impossible for me to guess how old he was. His body, lean and muscular, could pass for the body of a thirty year old, but his face looked much older. When I asked, Jubjub explained that Tcori didn't know his age. The Bushmen don't follow any sort of calendar, so they have no way of knowing how old they are. Bushmen, I guess, have no use for such information.

Tcori wore a tan cloth wrapped around his waist and a beaded necklace. Like his fellow Bushmen, his feet were small, coarse and bare. I couldn't imagine walking around the Kalahari without shoes. My feet would be torn to shreds before I'd taken ten steps. But after I watched Tcori walk over thorn bushes, jagged rocks and hot sand without even seeming to notice, I realized that a pair of shoes would be of no use to him. A lifetime of walking through the desert had hardened the soles of his feet until they had become as tough as leather.

The most fascinating thing about Tcori wasn't that he walked around barefoot. It was that he carried a spear. I kid you not. An honest-to-goodness spear. The neck of the spear was made from a Marula branch that had been shaved smooth. The arrow was carved out of elephant bone. I was told that Tcori was one of the last remaining hunters in his tribe.

After Tcori had been introduced to everyone, we learned that he had come to us with a message. While in the delta, he had been told that a poacher had shot and wounded a female lion. Making matters worse, Tcori said, was that the lioness had four young lion cubs. The lions were able to escape from the poacher, but he was tracking them and would surely finish the job if someone did not stop him.

There was no question in my mind–it was up to us to save the lions. I got so wound up, I jumped out of my seat.

"If we don't help them, who will?" I yelled. "You heard Tcori! The poacher will catch the lioness and her cubs before long, and when he does he'll kill them! We have no time to lose! We have to fly to the delta immediately!"

If Chocs hadn't settled me down, I would have probably jumped in a truck and sped off to the airstrip by myself. (I tend to react passionately when something is important to me...some people might even say I overreact.) Luckily, the rest of our group was more levelheaded. We all sat down in the dining tent and discussed our options.

Wyatt
Journal Entry Date: August 23
Location: Okavango Delta, Botswana
Time: 9:14 AM
Temperature: 14 Celsius, 60 Fahrenheit
Skies: Clearing
Wind: Light

Typically, humans shouldn't interact with wild animals under any circumstances. It's an unwritten law. In the wilderness, we must allow nature to take its course. But this is different. The lioness was shot by a poacher. And being shot illegally, with a high-powered rifle, is not an act of nature in my book. If the lioness had been injured in some other way, say, for example, she had broken her leg and was dying because she could not hunt for food, we would not get involved. That may seem cruel, but again, it's the law of nature, and we've learned that in Africa no animal ever dies in vain. They feed off one another. One animal's death helps another animal survive. It's the circle of life in action.

The lioness will not live long with a gunshot wound. This puts her cubs at great risk. For the first year of their lives, lion cubs feed on their mother's milk, and these cubs are only a few weeks old. If the mother dies, so will the cubs. Even if they are able to escape the poacher, they will face the danger of another predator. Most people think lions aren't challenged in the wild. But lions actually have an enemy who is strong enough to attack and kill them. That enemy is the hyena, and there are thousands of them on the delta.

FACT: Some wildlife experts estimate there to be fewer than 15,000 lions left in the wild today. Their numbers have decreased significantly since the early 1990s, when it was believed the lion population was over 100,000.

Chocs, Jubjub and Tcori are loading up a jeep with a week's worth of supplies: food, water, tents, sleeping bags and a medical kit. I also saw Chocs packing a rifle, which makes me a little nervous. I suppose it's better to have a rifle and not need it, than to need one and not have it. I'm always up for adventure, but our safari has turned into something much more serious.

Surprisingly, my parents gave the thumbs up for Gannon and me to go along, provided Chocs promises to keep us at a safe distance from the wildlife. Jubjub is going, too. She will stay at the main camp and act as our radio contact while we search for the lioness. The radio antenna at camp sends a signal as far as Maun, so Jubjub will be able to contact the authorities if we run into trouble.

I need to finish up this journal entry and check to make sure that I've packed all the necessary supplies. In less than an hour, we will make our way to the airstrip, where a pilot will be waiting to fly us to the central Okavango Delta. Once there, we will embark on an extremely dangerous mission that will test our strength and character. We are venturing into a hostile environment. There will be predators, snakes, disease-carrying insects and venomous spiders, any of which could bring our expedition to a disastrous end. I certainly hope we pass this test. Our lives depend on it.

Part III:

In Search of the Lioness and her Cubs

Gannon
Date: August 23
Location: High above the Okavango Delta

Flying over the Okavango Delta - Gannon

We've just passed over the delta's western edge. The colors of the landscape below us have changed from browns and reds to blues and greens. What an amazing contrast! The Kalahari is so barren, the delta so lush. I'd write more, but our plane is bouncing all over the sky, making it hard to take notes. Signing off until later....

Wyatt
Journal Entry Date: August 23
Location: Okavango Delta, Botswana
Time: 8:23 PM
Temperature: 18 Celsius, 68 Fahrenheit
Elevation: 3,021 feet above sea level
Skies: Hazy
Wind: Calm

Shinde Camp will be our base while we're in the delta. A small camp hidden in a forest, Shinde has a dozen or so large tents, a dining tent and a deck with a fire pit.

We arrived too late in the day to search for the lioness, so we decided to stay overnight at Shinde and go out at first light. As it got dark, we sat around a fire and listened as the nocturnal animals came to life all around us. Singing birds, howling baboons, laughing hippos and trumpeting elephants were all within earshot of camp. One thing is very clear—we are on the animals' turf now.

Chocs explained the differences between the Okavango Delta and the Kalahari.

"In the delta, wildlife is much more abundant than it is in the Kalahari," Chocs said. "Lions, hippos, elephants, leopards and cape buffalo can wander through your camp at any time. These animals are very active at night. So after dinner you will be escorted to your tent. Once you are in your tent, do not leave under any circumstances. If you venture out, you will be in danger. You may even hear animals walking past your tent during the night. Just keep quiet. They'll usually move along."

"Usually?" I said. "Well, what if they don't?"

"Don't worry," Chocs said with a laugh, "they almost always do."

Nothing against Chocs, but after the rhino attack, I find it hard to trust him. If the experience in the Kalahari taught us anything, it's that your safety is never guaranteed in the African bush.

Gannon
Location: Tent
Time: Early morning, still dark

Picture this: total darkness. So dark that you can't even see your hand two inches from your face. My brother and I lie on cots inside a small tent. Mosquito nets are draped over the cots to protect us from the bugs, and we have a thick down blanket to keep us warm. It's so quiet I can almost hear my heart beat. Thump-thump...thump-thump... thump-thump. The only other sound is a slight wind rustling through the trees.

Then, in the not-so-far-off distance, I hear what sounds like a roar. My heartbeat quickens. I look at the canvas walls of the tent and realize that they will do very little to stop a hungry predator from getting to us.

" Wyatt," I whisper, "are you awake?"

"Yes," he says.

"Did you hear that?"

"I did."

"What was it?"

"I don't know."

"Do you think it was a lion?"

"Probably."

"What do you mean, probably? What other animals roar like that?"

"None that I know of."

"So you think it was definitely a lion?"

"Yes. It was a lion, okay. Go to sleep."

"How am I supposed to sleep when I know there is a lion walking around outside our tent?"

"I don't know, Gannon."

Just then, I hear another roar, and then another.

"Oh, man. There's more than one lion, and it sounds like they're coming this way."

"I bet they're tracking your scent. Probably think you're a buffalo."

"I showered tonight. You're the one that

stinks."

"Go to sleep."

"Are you kidding? I'm not going to sleep a wink."

"Then why don't you go out there and shoo them away?"

"Very funny."

Inside each tent is a blow horn. These horns are left in the tents for "emergencies." If you have an emergency you are supposed to blow the horn. At the sound of the horn, an armed guard will come to your rescue. Or so we've been told.

Assuming that lions entering our tent to tear us from limb to limb would be considered an emergency, I take the blow horn off the shelf. With the horn in hand, I feel more prepared to fend off an attack, but then a thought crosses my mind: What if the horn doesn't work? What if I press the button and nothing happens? What if there is a manufacturing defect? What if this horn is a stinking dud? I curse myself for not testing the horn before nightfall. I think long and hard about blowing it for safe measure. "Why not?" I reason. "Better safe than sorry." But if I blow the horn, and the guard jumps from his bed and runs through the bush in his underpants only to find that there is not, in fact, an honest-to-goodness emergency, Chocs may begin to doubt that Wyatt and I are worthy of joining him on this expedition.

"Why did I bring these kids with me, anyway?" he might ask himself. "The Okavango Delta is no place for immature youngsters."

I don't want him to have that sort of impression of us. My brother and I have been in many frightening situations before, and given our experiences, I am confident that our bravery will measure up to that of the bravest teenager. But this is our first encounter with the king of the beasts, so I really don't know what to expect.

After awhile, the roars trail off in the distance and finally stop. I guess the lions chose to go after an animal with more meat on its bones, which is smart on the lions' part. Together, Wyatt and I would hardly qualify as an appetizer for a hungry lion. Still, just to make myself feel more comfortable, I keep the blow horn close all night, ready to sound that sucker at a moment's notice.

A male lion rests before the evening hunt - Gannon

Wyatt
Journal Entry Date: August 24
Location: Okavango Delta, Botswana
Time: 5:53 AM
Temperature: 4 Celsius, 40 Fahrenheit
Elevation: 3,021 feet above sea level
Skies: Hazy
Wind: Calm

I sit outside our tent, writing in my journal by the flickering light of a kerosene lantern. The sun hasn't come up yet, and it's cold. I am wrapped in a wool blanket and drinking hot chocolate that I made on our small camp stove. The benefit of colder weather is that there are fewer bugs. The Centers for Disease Control has the Okavango Delta listed as an official malaria area. I'm taking a malaria medication as a precaution, though I haven't seen a single mosquito since I got here.

I can hear some kind of animal moving through the bushes not far from where I sit. It is still too dark to make out what it is, but I do know this: it's BIG. I am sitting still in the hopes that I will not attract this animal's attention.

I slept decent last night, although I must admit, it is eerie to hear so many animals outside your tent. You lie there thinking to yourself, "What in the world is that? It sure sounds like something big, and if it's big, then that means it's also dangerous. Darn it, I just remembered that I left a candy bar in my backpack. How could I be so stupid? I hope the animal doesn't smell it and claw his way in for a snack."

Despite such nagging fears, we survived the night, and I was able to sleep four or five hours. I don't think Gannon slept a wink.

Today we will set off into the delta in search of the lioness. I have to admit, my nerves are beginning to get the better of me. It's always the waiting part that kills me. The sooner we leave, the better.

The sun is beginning to illuminate the delta

The elephant that was eating outside our tent
- Wyatt

wilderness. I can see just enough to make out the animal in the bushes nearby. It's a giant bull elephant...and I mean *GIANT!* His tusks have to weigh 100 pounds each! I'm remaining as still as possible, my only movement being my hand scribbling in my journal. I'll tell you, it's one thing to see an elephant at the zoo, but to see an elephant grazing on the bushes right next to your tent, well, that's a completely different experience.

Gannon
Time: Lunchtime
Location: Grassy plains

Loading into the jeep for our journey into the delta - Gannon

This morning at 6:15 we piled our supplies into the safari jeep, said good-bye to Jubjub and set off into the delta. There wasn't even time for us to eat breakfast, though Jubjub packed us each a bag of biscuits to take along. As Chocs said, "Every minute counts." We've been driving for a few hours and decided to stop for a morning snack.

I have to say, the remoteness of the delta is mind-blowing. Out here you feel so far away from the "real world." There are no cell phones out here in the bush, no TVs, no computers. I will not be watching the news, writing emails or surfing the Net. While in Botswana, I will have no idea what is going on in the outside world.

At first being in such a remote place felt strange. Without a TV, computer or cell phone, it seemed like there was nothing to do. I've become so used to having these things. But when you think about it, they're really nothing more than distractions. These days no one lives in the moment. It's almost like we're losing sight of things that are right in front of us.

My brother would probably quote Charles Darwin and say that we have "evolved." We are now used to these distractions. But in Africa, the rat race that exists in other parts of the world becomes insignificant. In Africa, you are forced to live in the moment, to notice the food you eat, to look at it and really taste it, rather than shovel it down while you try to finish five other things. You are forced to listen to a person speak until they have finished their thought, instead of interrupting them to answer a phone.

In Africa, you can really feel, hear and see things. You actually notice the breeze blowing through your hair. You hear the water flowing through the tall, green grass. You see the silver-backed spider crawling over the dusty ground. You are forced to notice these things because there is nothing to distract you.

Okay, enough with the philosophical mumbo-jumbo. Chocs just told us that it's time to get moving. Our journey continues....

Wyatt
Journal Entry Date: August 24
Location: Okavango Delta, Botswana
Time: 10:47 PM
Temperature: 14 Celsius, 60 Fahrenheit
Skies: Clear
Wind: Calm

I can't believe how much wildlife there is in the Okavango Delta! Elephants, zebras, wildebeests, giraffes, warthogs, impala, hippos and cape buffalos, all by the dozens!

I was so overwhelmed by the incredible number of animals we saw today, I almost forgot about the poor lioness.

FACT: Scientists estimate that there are as many as 260,000 large mammals and 500 bird species in the Okavango Delta.

But every now and then Chocs would stop the jeep and Tcori would step out and quietly move through the bush to look at something in the grass or pick up something from the ground or check the markings on a tree. Tcori learned to track animals from his ancestors in the Kalahari. Watching him work was a reminder that we weren't on your typical safari.

Just before sundown, Tcori tore several branches and leaves from a bush and put them in his satchel.

"Inside that bush is a sticky sap that can be smeared on an arrowhead and used as poison," Chocs explained.

"But why does Tcori need poison?" Gannon asked. "We're not going to kill any animals, are we?"

"A small dose of the poison will not kill a large animal," Chocs explained, "but it is powerful enough to knock the animal unconscious. Tcori will use this poison on the lioness so that she will sleep while we remove the bullet."

I'd never thought about how we would remove the bullet from the lioness, but I suppose she wouldn't just allow us to walk right up and start poking around her wound. Keeping her unconscious is not only the safe thing to do, it's also the humane thing to do.

Shortly before dark, we set up an overnight camp–four tents in some flat grass near a narrow waterway. The type of tent we are using has two tarps, each hanging over a wooden frame in the shape of an upside down "V." The larger tarp goes on top, providing shade and protecting us from bad weather. The smaller tarp hangs underneath the larger tarp, allowing just enough space for one person to sleep.

After putting up the tents, we had a simple dinner of rice and beans, and a cup of hot tea. There is something about camping that makes any food taste good, no matter how boring the meal. This dinner was no exception.

After dinner, everyone else settled into their tents. But I stayed up, sitting alone by the campfire, enjoying the incredible night sky. The fact that Chocs had a rifle in his tent lessened my fears somewhat, but the truth is, I was still a bit jumpy. When a warthog sprang from the nearby bushes I was so startled I ran to my tent faster than you can say "goodnight."

A family of hippos feeds along the river bank
- Wyatt

Gannon
Journal Entry Date: August 25
Time: 3:21 AM

For the second straight night, I cannot sleep! I'm inside my tent, tucked into my sleeping bag, but wide awake. I've tried everything to quiet my mind. I even tried counting sheep, but it's no use. Every time I close my eyes, I see the beady, black eyes of a vulture staring at me. Let me explain.

After lunch we continued our journey, passing almost every animal imaginable as we drove. During the drive, I felt calm. There was no sense of danger. We were safe. But in the late afternoon, when Tcori jumped from the jeep to scout a possible location for our camp, he suddenly stopped dead in his tracks. Something high above had caught his eye. I looked up to see what it was. Perched directly above us was a vulture.

There's really no nice way to say it, so I'll just be honest: vultures are hideous creatures. In case you've never seen one, I included a photo I took so you have an idea of what I'm talking about.

The way this vulture looked at us sent chills down my spine, and I couldn't help but think it was a bad sign. After spotting the vulture, Tcori told Chocs that we had to find another location to camp for the night. Something about that vulture had bothered Tcori, that's for sure, and if something bothers Tcori, it bothers me.

Before we left, I took out my video camera and filmed the ugly old bird, trying my best to get a nice, steady close-up. I was happy with the footage, but as we drove on, the menacing gaze of the bird kept appearing in my mind. When we finally stopped for the night, I jotted down this short poem.

If you ever stare into the eyes of a vulture,
You may find,
Within the darkness,

A frightening trick of the mind.
In the bird's pupil,
The reflection of a tomb.
A sign that just around the corner,
Awaits one's doom.

It is now close to 4:00 AM, and I am still awake and restless, very much afraid of what dangers might lie in our path.

The vulture that inspired my poem - Gannon

Wyatt
Journal Entry Date: August 25
Location: Okavango Delta, Botswana
Time: 9:32 AM
Temperature: 14 Celsius, 60 Fahrenheit
Skies: Hazy
Wind: Calm

Early this morning, disaster struck. Not far from camp we came upon a waterway that was approximately three hundred feet wide from shore to shore. Chocs said he'd driven through this stretch of water many times in the past and assured us that the vehicle would have no problem reaching the other side.

"These safari jeeps are built for this sort of travel," he said. "The engine is sealed off, and the snorkel extends four feet higher so that the engine can draw enough air to operate even when it's completely underwater."

Chocs confidently drove the jeep into the water without a second thought. The first thirty yards or so were smooth going. It reminded me of being in a boat. A low wake trailed behind us. Then the water got deeper, and it began to pour over the jeep's side, filling the interior. I lifted my feet onto the seat to keep my shoes from getting drenched. As the water got deeper, the jeep started to look like a submarine trolling on the surface of the ocean. Only the seats and roll bars were above the water line. But still, the engine trudged on.

"When I'm old enough to drive, I want a jeep just like this one," Gannon said.

"Me too," I said. "Think of the adventures we could go on in the Rocky Mountains."

As Gannon and I dreamed of one day having our own safari jeeps, our vehicle jolted to a stop. Chocs jumped up on the seat and looked over the hood.

"Uh-oh," he said.

"Uh-oh?" I repeated. "That doesn't sound good."

"We've hit something," he said.

"A hippo?" Gannon asked.

"If it were a hippo, he would have flipped the jeep by now. It's probably just a rock."

Chocs backed up and tried to go around whatever was blocking our path, but again the vehicle came to a sudden stop.

"I'm going in for a closer look," Chocs said and waded into the water. He moved to the front of the vehicle and sank underneath. After a good thirty seconds, he came back up, wiping water from his face.

"There's a tree trunk under the water," he said. "It's too big to go over it. We'll go downstream and see if we can drive around it."

But when we backed up, the wheels lost their traction and started to spin. Chocs tried everything he could, but the jeep wasn't going anywhere. Then to make matters worse, the engine died. Chocs tried several times to restart it, but it was no use.

"Grab your things," Chocs said. "It looks like we're going to have to swim for it."

I had a slight problem with this plan, but it had nothing to do with the swimming part. I could swim. The problem was the giant crocodile sleeping on the shore. Without question, this was the biggest croc I'd ever seen. I kid you not. It had to be fifteen feet long! Chocs said that if we kept quiet and didn't splash around too much, the croc probably wouldn't wake up.

"He probably won't wake up?" I said. "Well for sake of argument, let's just say that he does? Then what?"

"If the croc wakes up," Chocs said with a smile, "just swim faster."

His answer didn't comfort me in the least. Even if the sleeping croc didn't wake up, who's to say that one of his buddies wasn't hiding just under the water's surface somewhere nearby? Despite my apprehension, we were stuck dead smack in the middle of the waterway. What other choice did we have but to swim?

FACT: Crocodiles feed mostly on fish but are also known to eat birds, zebras, wildebeest, hippos and, on rare occasions, humans. They can grow to well over fifteen feet in length, can swim up to fifteen miles per hour and often live to be more than eighty years old.

"We're swimming to that beach," Chocs said as he pointed to a beachhead approximately one hundred and fifty feet from where we sat in the stalled jeep.

We gathered our supplies and loaded them into three waterproof duffels. With our supplies sealed off, we waded into the water. The water in the delta was crystal clear. Where we stood, it was nearly chest deep. I began moving quietly through the water, slipping along the muddy bottom toward shore.

I hadn't been in the water thirty seconds when I felt something slam into my shoulder. My worst fear was suddenly realized. A croc was attacking!

I screamed for help and spun around to fight for my life. Behind me I saw the long, spiny back of a giant croc floating just above the water's surface. I swung my fist down on top of it again and again, screaming all the while.

Somehow in the middle of my panic, I

remembered having read about a guy who survived an attack by poking the croc in the eyes. As I searched frantically for an eye to gouge, I realized that the creature I was battling wasn't actually a croc at all. In fact, it wasn't even a creature. It was, much to my relief, a log. Can you believe it? A big, slimy log!

My relief quickly turned into humiliation. I felt so foolish for fighting a harmless piece of bark. Even worse, Gannon saw the whole thing. He was laughing so hard he could barely breathe. And I know from past experiences that he'll never let me hear the end of it. I'm not kidding. We'll be ninety years old, relaxing on the front porch in our favorite rocking chairs, and he'll say, "Hey, Wyatt. You remember that time in Botswana when you were so savagely attacked by that log?"

But there was no time to stew over my brother's amusement. I hadn't even caught my breath when I heard Chocs yell.

"The croc's awake! Swim for it, boys!"

I turned just in time to see the giant croc waddling into the water. All of my yelling and splashing woke him up, and he didn't seem too happy about it. We all swam as fast as we could toward the shore, but the croc was closing in on us fast, its tail slithering like a snake in the calm water. When you're being chased by a croc, it feels like you're moving in super-duper slow motion, regardless of how fast you're actually swimming. Luckily, we were swimming just fast enough. When we finally climbed ashore the croc was still a good fifty feet behind us.

Floating on top of the water just off shore, he stared at us as if to say, "You got lucky this time, but I wouldn't try it again if I were you."

Don't worry, Mr. Croc. We won't.

One of the many crocs that call the Okavango home - Wyatt

Gannon
Journal Entry Date: August 25
Time: 3:32 PM

After rolling around on shore laughing hysterically at my brother, it dawned on me: we had a very serious situation on our hands. Our transportation was stuck in the middle of a waterway, and there was no way to get it out. Chocs radioed Jubjub at camp.

"Chocs to Shinde Camp. Come in, Shinde."

"Jubjub here. How is everything going?"

"Not so good. The jeep is stuck in deep water. We need someone to drive the other jeep to us so we can pull it out."

"Well," Jubjub said, "I hate to tell you this, but I'm afraid that's not possible."

As luck would have it, the other jeep was broken down. A mechanic was working on the engine, but Jubjub said it needed several new parts that would have to be flown in from Maun. At best, the jeep would be fixed in four days.

"Okay, Jubjub," Chocs said. "I suppose there's nothing more you can do. Keep us posted on the progress of the vehicle. I'll radio you again later."

"Okay, Dad. Be safe out there."

"I will. I love you."

"Love you, too. Over and out."

Chocs set down the radio and turned to us.

"Well, gentlemen," he said very matter-of-factly. "It looks like we're on our own. From here on out, we'll travel by foot."

Being on foot in the bush increases the level of danger a thousand fold. When you are in a truck, animals view the vehicle and all of its passengers as one very large animal and, thus, are unlikely to attack. But on foot, you are just a small human being. However, despite our obvious disadvantage in strength, most animals, including the fiercest predators, view humans as a threat and usually avoid confrontation. Again, there are exceptions to the rule, and those exceptions are what worry me.

Before we set off on our trek, Chocs translated as Tcori passed on some important bush wisdom.

"If we encounter a lion," he said, "do not run. Even if the lion charges, do not run. It is most likely a mock charge, meaning the lion is only trying to size you up and see if you are really a threat. In this case, a lion will halt his charge and turn away. But if you run, the lion will chase you, and if that happens you're in trouble. What you need to do is keep eye contact with the lion and back away slowly. If you try to hide behind a tree or lie down, a lion might become curious and move in for a closer look, and if that happens you're in trouble as well."

"Just to make sure I understand this correctly," I said, "the idea is to stay out of trouble."

"Precisely," Chocs said with a toothy grin.

I have to say, if a lion does charge I'm not so sure I'll be able to hold my ground. Isn't it human nature to run from something that can tear you limb from limb? I just hope that I'm able to remember this advice and not freak out like Wyatt did when he encountered the tree-stump croc.

To improve my chances of reacting like you're supposed to in the face of a lion, I made up a little saying that I will repeat quietly to myself as we walk. It goes like this: "Stay calm, keep eye contact and back away slowly...." Repeat. My hope is that if I say it enough it will become ingrained in my mind and I'll react appropriately.

Regardless of the dangers, the aspiring filmmaker in me can't help but view this trek as an opportunity. Imagine how amazing it would be to capture a charging lion on film. That kind of footage would put me in the ranks of some of the great wildlife filmmakers of all time. That is, if I could keep my hands from shaking so much that it would look like I was filming an earthquake.

Knowing that Chocs has a rifle and that he and Tcori have a lifetime of experience in the bush gives me confidence that we will actually survive this journey. Both of these men know how to navigate the African wilderness, and more importantly, how to behave around animals. Without this knowledge, you quickly fall a few notches on the food chain.

We all agree that abandoning the jeep was probably a blessing in disguise. Because the lioness was shot by a poacher driving a truck, she would likely run at the first sound of an approaching vehicle. On foot, Tcori said, we have a much better chance of finding and helping the lioness and her four cubs.

In a few minutes, we will continue moving south until an hour or so before dusk. That's when we'll scout out a good location to set up camp and stay the night. Despite our optimism in the face of our latest challenge, the eerie image of that vulture lingers in my mind.

Wyatt
Journal Entry Date: August 25
Location: Okavango Delta, Botswana
Time: 11:47 PM
Temperature: 13 Celsius, 58 Fahrenheit
Skies: Clear
Wind: Light

I am awake and, to be completely honest, not feeling as strong as I would like. I think the day's excitement, combined with the long trek through the bush, has sapped me of all my energy. It is difficult even to write, but I must take a moment to document our encounter with the elephants earlier today.

While walking from the dusty, barren landscape into a forested riverbed, we encountered for the first time the sad and destructive consequences of poaching. Under the cool shade of the trees, we saw a female elephant lying on her side with a severe wound to her right hind leg. She had stepped into a poacher's trap, and a wire snare was wrapped tightly around the lower part of her leg. The snare had torn through the elephant's tough skin, and the wound had become terribly infected. The elephant could no longer walk.

Tcori said there was nothing we could do. This poor elephant was dying, and it was only a matter of time before the scavengers moved in to feast on her remains. Once the scavengers had done their job, the poacher would return to collect the tusks. In an effort to prevent this, Chocs radioed the elephant's coordinates to Jubjub, who, in turn, radioed the authorities. It is the practice of the government to remove a dead elephant's tusks and store them in a vault. They do this to keep the tusks out of the poachers' hands.

A large bull elephant circled the female elephant like he was a husband in mourning. With his tusks, the bull tried desperately to lift his companion. It was as if the bull would not accept the fate of his mate. It even appeared that the bull was crying.

> FACT: *Temporal glands located just behind the eyes excrete a fluid when an elephant becomes stressed. This fluid, which streams down the side of an elephant's face, closely resembles tears.*

To me, the tears were proof that the bull elephant was sad. People think animals don't feel. That's not true; animals do feel and some, like the elephant, show great emotion.

With that, I must now finish this entry. I am feeling weaker and more feverish with each passing minute. I must get some rest if I hope to feel stronger by morning.

Gannon
Journal Entry Date: August 26
Time: 11:01 AM

It's official. There is no disputing it. Just as I thought, the vulture was a bad omen. Our expedition is cursed!

Wyatt is very sick. He woke up this morning with a high fever. He was pale and had the chills. Before our trip, my mother told us about the different illnesses people can come down with in Africa. Given this knowledge, we took steps to protect ourselves. For example, we're taking malaria medication, so we have eliminated the possibility that Wyatt contracted malaria. We were also vaccinated for hepatitis A and B, polio, typhoid and yellow fever.

However, there are several illnesses that have no vaccination. Dengue fever, which is transmitted by mosquitoes, is one example. But we've seen very few mosquitoes since we arrived. I thought that Wyatt might have been bitten by a tsetse fly, as I had read that these flies are found throughout Sub-Saharan Africa. A bite from one of these bumblebee-sized insects can cause "African sleeping sickness," a serious illness that causes fatigue, aching muscles and joints, and severe headaches. Wyatt has all of these symptoms, but Chocs informed me that tsetse flies were eradicated from Botswana years ago.

Other than insects, there are bacteria in the delta water that can make you sick. This bacteria doesn't bother the natives. They have grown up drinking the water and are used to it. But the bacteria are foreign to us and can cause intestinal problems if swallowed. As a precaution, we've been boiling our drinking water, which kills most bacteria and viruses. We also have a small supply of iodine tablets, which we use to purify the water when we don't have time to boil it. Wyatt and I haven't had a drop of untreated water, which leaves us scratching our heads. As is the case with many illnesses in Africa, we are unable to come up with an accurate diagnosis.

With Wyatt being too weak to travel, our search for the lioness has been delayed. However, Tcori spent much of the morning in the bush. Apparently, he found signs of the lioness and her cubs and is confident that we will find them soon.

But at the moment, the most important thing is Wyatt's health. He must rest and regain his strength if we hope to complete our mission.

If his condition worsens, we will have to abandon our search. There are no doctors in the bush. When you get sick out here, you're on your own. If the situation gets bad enough, however, Jubjub can ask the authorities in Maun to call for an airlift to the capital city of Gaborone, where there is a hospital. I hope it doesn't come to this. If it does, that means Wyatt's life would be in danger.

The following was scribbled on Wyatt's map in the early morning hours of August 27. The note was found by Gannon sometime later.

Should I die on this journey, I want my family to know that I have had a fun and adventurous life, and that I love them.... Wyatt

Gannon
Time: The middle of the night

I am in Wyatt's tent so that I can monitor him during the night. His temperature has been between 103 and 105 degrees for several hours. That's no laughing matter as far as body temperature is concerned. Prolonged high fever can cause brain damage or worse. He's sleeping at the moment, but just recently he had severe hallucinations and what appeared to be a seizure.

The things he has been saying for the last few hours make absolutely no sense. At one point, he was having a conversation with our grandfather who died about five years ago. I shook him, trying desperately to break him from this crazy dream state, but he wouldn't come to. It was like he was possessed.

As frightening as the hallucinations were, his seizure was downright horrifying. Without warning, his arms curled up, as if they were seized by cramps, and his neck muscles stiffened. He made an awful noise, as if he was trying to clear his throat, and then he started shaking violently. That's when his eyes began to roll back in his head.

"Stay with me, Wyatt!" I yelled. "Stay with me!"

In a panic, I ripped off my belt, folded it over and shoved it between his teeth so he wouldn't bite off his tongue. Forcing his mouth open with the belt seemed to clear his airway. Once he began breathing regularly, he relaxed and fell into a deep sleep.

The hospital in Gaborone has been notified, but they cannot send a helicopter until morning. Jubjub is on standby and will update the hospital with Wyatt's condition at 5:30 AM. If Wyatt needs to be evacuated, they will send a chopper, which can be here within a couple hours. But I'm terrified he won't make it to morning. His breathing is all over the place. Sometimes his breaths are short and quick, other times he won't inhale for ten or fifteen seconds. Whenever this happens, I am afraid that I'm watching my brother die right before my eyes. It sends me into a panic. I hit him on the chest, smack his face, scream at him...anything to get him to breathe. Once he does, I collapse with relief.

It's such a helpless feeling, knowing there is nothing I can do to help Wyatt. I'll tell you, it's crazy the way an illness puts your feelings for someone in perspective. I mean, some days my brother aggravates me so much I swear I could kill him. But now that he's really in danger, I'd literally do anything to save him.

I can't help but regret leaving our parents in the Kalahari to join Chocs and Tcori on this expedition. It was a terrible, terrible decision.

Gannon
Time: 4:47 AM

I've been up all night watching my brother and watching the clock. This whole ordeal has been incredibly stressful. I must have stuck my finger under Wyatt's nose to see if he was breathing at least a thousand times, but it seems he recently made a turn. At least, I hope so.

About thirty minutes ago, Wyatt's face became flushed and beaded up with sweat. Soon after, his face returned to a normal color. I wiped away the sweat and felt his forehead. It was a lot cooler.

He was conscious for a few minutes and able to answer questions with a simple nod or shake of the head. When I asked him if he felt any better, he actually nodded "yes." This illness has taken its toll, but I really think that the worst is behind us.

Gannon
Time: 5:42 AM

Just after 5:00 AM, Wyatt sat up and drank a half cup of tea. He even said "good morning" when Chocs came into the tent. These may seem like little things, but they're a huge improvement for Wyatt. Chocs relieved me of my watch and ordered me to get some rest, an order I will gladly obey.

Wyatt
Journal Entry Date: August 27
Location: Okavango Delta, Botswana
Time: 7:24 PM
Temperature: 13 Celsius, 58 Fahrenheit
Skies: Cloudy
Wind: Light

I write this journal entry as I'm seated beside a warm, crackling campfire. My hands are still a bit shaky, but the fact that I am writing is a good sign. As you know, writing takes a good amount of mental energy. The fact that I even want to write is proof that I am on the mend.

During the worst of my illness, I became desperate for relief and asked Tcori if the Bushmen had any natural remedies for a fever. Tcori assured me that they did and went about gathering roots and leaves from an assortment of shrubs. He boiled them all in a pot, put the steaming concoction inside my tent and told me to take long, deep breaths. Other than clearing my nasal passages, I don't know that this remedy did me any good. In fact, my headache actually got worse, and I became nauseous. Whether this was a result of the treatment or not is impossible to know. Not wanting to discredit Tcori's traditional medicine or offend him in any way, I simply thanked him for going to such great lengths to help me.

After Tcori's treatment, I slept on and off throughout the night. I woke up drenched in sweat just before sunrise, but I felt much better. Chocs radioed Jubjub and let her know that my condition had improved. He felt I was on the road to recovery but asked Jubjub to keep the medical evacuation helicopter on alert, just in case.

I do, however, think it's safe to say that I will live to see another day. Though I must confess, at times I had my doubts. From what I've been told, so did everyone else.

When I was shivering inside my tent, I was reminded of *Missionary Travels in Southern Africa*, by Dr. David Livingstone, a book I had read before our trip. In his journals he describes a seven-month expedition from the Zambezi River to the west coast of Africa. During this expedition his crew experienced no fewer than thirty-one cases of fever, and by the time they reached the coast, most of the men had severe dysentery. Many years later, Dr. Livingstone himself died on an expedition in Zambia from internal bleeding caused by malaria and dysentery. Knowing the nature of the seemingly indestructible explorer's death made me even more worried about myself. If the perils of the African wilderness were too much for someone as tough as Dr. Livingstone, what chance did I have?

I suppose I'm just lucky that my illness was somehow cured. What doesn't kill you makes you stronger, right? And I do feel stronger and plan to continue my research with a renewed spirit. As the famous naturalist Charles Darwin once wrote, "A man who dares to waste one hour of time has not discovered the value of life." I wouldn't be surprised if Mr. Darwin had jotted this down after being laid up in bed with the flu. That's the irony of illness. It gives you a renewed appreciation for life.

Let the journey continue....

Gannon
Journal Entry Date: August 27
Time: 8:52 PM

"Jubjub to Father. Come in, Father. How is Wyatt?"

This was the radio call that woke me up mid-afternoon.

"Hello, Jubjub," Chocs said. "He is doing much better. We plan to continue our search first thing tomorrow morning."

"That's wonderful news."

"You can notify the hospital that we won't be needing the helicopter. And please radio Wyatt's parents to let them know that he is okay."

"I will let everyone know right away!"

Boy, I can't tell you how relieved I was to hear this. Still wiped out from the experience, I stayed in my tent for a while, just enjoying the sound of everyone's voices outside. When I finally came out, it was time to make dinner. But first I had to give Wyatt a solid punch in the arm for putting me through that whole ordeal.

"It's good to see you, too," he said.

"Next time you pull something like that," I said, "I'm going to save myself the hassle and just feed you to the animals."

I was starving and helped gather sticks for a fire, stopping briefly to watch a herd of elephants move slowly across the horizon.

Over dinner we discussed our plan. I thought for sure that Wyatt would vote to call off the expedition and return to Edo's Camp in the Kalahari. After being so sick, it would have been understandable. But my brother is stubborn. He wants to finish what we came to do. And so do I.

Once it was dark, we gathered around the campfire and watched as Tcori carved a bow and several arrows from the tree branches he had collected. When he finished carving his last arrow, he placed them above the fire to cure and vanished into the darkness.

I think I should hit the sack. Despite sleeping

most of the day, I'm completely exhausted. Last night really rattled my nerves. I'm hoping that a full night of sleep will help me feel normal again. We resume our trek in the morning.

Gannon
Journal Entry Date: August 28
Time: 7:47 AM

So much for a full night of sleep. It seems ridiculous now, but one of the animals I was anxious to see in Africa was a baboon. I don't know why. It was just something about them, like the way they go about their business as if no one else on earth matters. Before our trip, I saw a video of a family barbeque in South Africa being ambushed by baboons. The family threw things at the baboons to scare them away, but the baboons kept coming back to stuff their bellies until they were full.

You'd think that someone with this knowledge would stash their food away in a safe place before they went to bed for the night. But no, I left my food outside like an idiot. Sure enough, just as I was falling asleep, I heard a ruckus outside my tent. I then made the mistake of sticking my head through the tent door and found myself face to face with the king of all baboons–if, in fact, baboons have kings.

Not knowing what else to do, I said something like, "Hey there, big fella." Well, he didn't like that too much and took a hard swipe at my face with his hand. Luckily he missed, and I quickly retreated into my tent.

When you camp, you should keep your food in an animal-proof container, something that is airtight so animals can't pick up the scent. I was upset with myself for being so careless, but Chocs made me feel a little better this morning when he said, "You're lucky it was baboons that came for your food instead of hyenas. If it was hyenas, they would have eaten you, too."

I'm going to have to agree with Chocs on that one.

A hyena on the hunt for his next meal...luckily it wasn't me - Gannon

Wyatt
Journal Entry Date: August 28
Location: Okavango Delta, Botswana
Time: 7:53 AM
Temperature: 12 Celsius, 56 Fahrenheit
Skies: Partly Cloudy
Wind: 5-10 mph

I was told Gannon probably saved my life the other night when I had a seizure, but this morning I could kill him with my bare hands! Thanks to the dinner party he threw for the baboons, our food supply has been seriously diminished. If we hope to continue our mission, we'll have to depend on Chocs and Tcori to find food on the delta. I'm hoping that won't be a problem, as Tcori has lived off the land his entire life. But it will definitely slow our search for the lioness, as much of our time will now be spent finding food. It's just one more obstacle we must overcome, but I suppose that's the nature of adventure.

Wyatt
Journal Entry Date: August 28
Location: Okavango Delta, Botswana
Time: 12:09 PM
Temperature: 24 Celsius, 80 Fahrenheit
Skies: Gathering storms to the north
Wind: 15-20 mph

As it turns out, the baboon debacle was not without its benefits. Since we had to clean up their mess, we were an hour or so behind schedule. If we'd left on time, it's likely that we would not have crossed paths with the cape buffalos!

Saying that we "crossed paths" is really misleading. It would be more accurate to say that · we were surrounded by them. Having just passed through a stretch of woods, we noticed a dust cloud on the horizon. We climbed up a small dune for a closer look and saw a herd of cape buffalos stretching across the plains as far as we could see. Chocs estimated there were at least 500 buffalos, and suddenly, every one of them was looking right at us. Imagine 1,000 buffalo eyes staring right at you! Intimidating, and that's putting it mildly.

My dad says cape buffalos have a look that says, "Don't mess with me, sucker!" and he's right. They are known to be one of the toughest and most aggressive animals in Africa. They kill more than a few humans each year and can even put up a fight against a lion.

I quickly snapped a few photos. But as the herd moved closer, I decided to put away the camera. I thought the sound of the camera's shutter opening and closing might cause a stampede. One of the buffalos, a large male, took a few quick steps toward us and then stopped. It was as if he was reminding us that they were in charge. Not that we needed a reminder. We knew darn well.

Chocs and Tcori whispered to remain calm and not make any sudden movements.

"Cape buffalos are most aggressive when they are alone," Chocs said, without moving a muscle. "That's when predators take advantage and attack them. As a herd they feel safe, so they're not likely to harm us as long as we keep quiet."

Just then, Gannon whispered to Chocs.

"What if I feel a sneeze coming on?" he said.

"Do you feel one coming on?" Chocs asked.

"I think so."

"Try your best to hold it."

"That's going to be difficult."

"Gannon," I said in a deadly serious tone, "I don't care if you have to hold your breath for the next ten minutes. You better not sneeze."

Now, a normal sneeze may go unnoticed by such a large herd, but a Gannon sneeze, well, that's different. When Gannon sneezes it's like a Category 5 hurricane just blew ashore. He could literally blow the stink off a pig. I was afraid it would scare the buffalos half to death and get us all trampled. Gannon closed his eyes tight and plugged his nose with his fingers. His face turned blood red, and veins bulged in his forehead. We all held our breath, fearing the worst. It looked like his head was about to explode. Then all of a sudden, he dropped his hands and whispered calmly, "We're good. Sneeze went away."

The herd walked by at a leisurely pace, their rough hides scratching us as they passed. With the exception of a few snorts here and there, they showed no signs of aggression. It was like they were out on a casual morning stroll, one buffalo blindly following another. Within ten minutes, they had all disappeared into the bush. About ten minutes after that, I finally stopped shaking.

A tense standoff with a massive herd of cape buffalos - Wyatt

Gannon
Journal Entry Date: Don't know, don't care
Time: Lunchtime

I've always thought of snakes as a reptile to be avoided at all costs, but today Tcori actually went in search of one.

We'd just stopped for a rest when Tcori set off.

"Where is he going?" I asked Chocs.

"To find some lunch," he answered.

"What are we having for lunch?" I asked hesitantly.

"That depends on what he finds," Chocs answered. "Let's build a fire."

Collecting dry sticks for the fire, I watched as Tcori looked into various holes and burrows at the base of several trees. Chocs, Wyatt and I were filling a shallow pit with our wood when I noticed Tcori poking a stick deep into one of the holes. When he stood up, a large, black snake slithered from the hole, obviously aggravated by Tcori's prodding. The snake rose up and threatened to strike, but the reptile didn't have a chance. Swiping his stick, Tcori pinned the snake to the ground, held it steady and chopped off its head with his blade. Gruesome, to say the least.

He then carried the long body to us and

dropped it near the pit. The snake was at least nine feet long, with shiny black scales.

"I hope that's not the lunch you were talking about," I said.

"Yes, it is," Chocs said with a smile.

"What kind of snake is it?" I asked.

"Black mamba," Chocs said.

"When we were in the Kalahari, Jubjub told us black mambas are poisonous," I said.

"Extremely poisonous."

"And we're going to eat it?" I asked, confused.

"Absolutely. The meat is delicious!"

Chocs explained that the venom is stored in a sack located in the back of the snake's head. As I mentioned, Tcori had already cut off the head, so, technically, the snake was safe to eat. But before you cook a snake, there is more work to be done than simply cutting off the head. Tcori took his knife and made an incision along the belly that ran the length of the snake. He then took a firm hold of the skin and peeled it off, exposing the snake's pinkish meat. Finally, he removed the guts of the snake and tossed them to the ground.

As Tcori cooked the black mamba, its pasty meat crackling over the fire, I didn't think I'd be able to stomach a single bite. But trekking through the bush you work up quite an appetite, and by the time the snake meat was cooked, I was ravenous. Tcori cut the snake into six-inch sections and handed a piece to each of us. I had never eaten snake, so I set my portion on my lap and watched as Tcori and Chocs peeled strips of meat away from the bones and tossed them into their mouths.

"Mmm," Chocs said. "Very good. Try it, Gannon and Wyatt. I think you'll like it."

Wyatt and I looked at each other, neither of us believing that we'd actually enjoy the taste of snake. I mean, if snake is so good, why isn't it served in restaurants? Reluctantly, I peeled a small strip of meat and quickly tossed it in my mouth. Hard to believe, but it actually tasted decent. All right, fine, I'll confess. Chocs was right. The snake was delicious.

"It tastes a lot like chicken," I said.

After swallowing his first bite, Wyatt agreed.

"Not bad," he said. "Not bad at all."

"Did you doubt me?" Chocs asked.

"Of course, we doubted you," I said, and we all laughed.

Our enjoyment of the black mamba probably had a lot to do with the fact that we were starving. When you're starving, almost anything tastes good. It's time to get going. Thunderclouds are gathering north of us. It's important that we make ground while the weather permits.

Wyatt
Journal Entry Date: August 28
Location: Okavango Delta, Botswana
Time: 5:58 PM
Temperature: 18 Celsius, 68 Fahrenheit
Skies: Thunderstorms
Wind: 15-20 mph

The rain has made it very difficult to trek any farther today and impossible to track the lioness. This is unfortunate because we were close. Just as the thunder began to rumble and black clouds moved overhead, we heard a roar in the distance. It was clear by our smiles that we were all thinking the same thing: *"That's her!"*

But just then the skies opened up and we experienced a downpour that would have sent Noah running for his ark. Not having an ark, we ran for some trees along a dried riverbed and quickly put up a tarp for shelter. Water soon flowed in the riverbed, turning the hill where we sat into a small island.

"This will be a good place to stay the night," Chocs said. "We're high enough from the water that our camp won't flood. And like the red lechwe, we can use the water to warn us of approaching predators."

I asked Chocs to explain.

"Red lechwes are a species of antelope," said Chocs. "They like to gather on islands and use the water as a warning system. As predators close in, the lechwes hear them splashing and know that danger is approaching. Lechwes are very fast in shallow water and can outrun the predator if they get a good head start. On dry land, they might not hear the predator until it's too late."

How smart, I thought. It's amazing what you can learn from animals.

FACT: *There are over 30,000 red lechwes living in the wetlands of the Okavango Delta.*

"What's the safest place to stay when you're trekking in the African bush?" I asked. "On an

A Red Lechwe on high alert for predators - Wyatt

island? In a tree? On the open plain?"

"In a hotel, if you can find one," Chocs said, followed by that great laugh of his.

Gannon
Journal Entry Date: Irrelevant
Time: Morning

This morning, Chocs woke me just after sunrise. "Gannon," he whispered. "Come out of your tent and do it quietly."

"What now?" I thought. "We're probably surrounded by a pod of hungry hippos."

I put on my boots and slowly opened the tent door, trying my best not to make any noise. When I poked my head outside I saw Wyatt, Chocs and Tcori looking up into the tree that spread out over our camp. About fifty feet above us was one of the most elusive creatures on earth, the leopard. Leopards are known for their sharp vision and radar-like hearing, and they typically flee at the first sight of a human. Because of this, it's very rare to see one. This beautiful cat, however, seemed perfectly at ease around us, casually grooming its spotted coat with steady laps of its long, pink tongue.

Tcori spoke, and Chocs translated. "This leopard has eaten recently," Chocs said. "You can still see the blood around its mouth. As long as we don't do anything to make the leopard feel that it is in danger, we'll be okay."

We slowly packed up camp without saying much of anything to each other. The leopard was watching us, studying our every move. Once I was packed, I grabbed my camera to take some video, but when I looked up in the tree, the leopard was gone.

"Where did it go?" I whispered. We all looked around but didn't see it anywhere. Like a phantom in the night, it had vanished.

About fifteen minutes later, we were completely packed and ready to begin the day's trek. That's when I spotted the leopard. He hadn't

The leopard that slept in the tree above our camp - Gannon

disappeared after all. He'd just moved without making a sound.

"Wyatt," I whispered. "Turn around slowly. He's right behind you."

Just across the shallow riverbed sat the leopard, licking his paw under the shade of a tree. Wyatt backed away slowly, readied his camera and snapped some photos. I grabbed my video camera and began filming. We kept at it until the leopard grew tired of our gawking, stood up and casually strolled away.

Wyatt
Journal Entry Date: August 29
Location: Okavango Delta, Botswana
Time: 6:51 PM
Temperature: 15 Celsius, 62 Fahrenheit
Skies: Clear
Wind: 5 mph
Number of predators in a one-mile radius: Tons

As I write this journal entry, I am resting against the trunk of a tree, just happy to be in one piece. Our bravery was just put to the ultimate test, and to be honest, I nearly cracked under the pressure. I only hope that when all is said and done, we make it out of the bush alive. But we're beginning to push our luck.

There are countless stories of explorers dying in Africa. The most famous story of all, Dr. Livingstone, I've already mentioned. But the great Dr. Livingstone wasn't the only one. There are many others, such as Keith Johnston, the Scottish cartographer (that's someone who makes maps), who died of dysentery in the first weeks of his expedition to map the central lakes of Africa. Then there's Mungo Park, who was murdered by tribesmen while on a mission to find the source of the Niger River. Another forty men on Park's expedition died from complications of malaria.

The list goes on–Clapperton, Lander and Tuckey, just to name a few. Now, we don't have to worry about blood-thirsty tribesmen these days, but there are other skillful killers that still wander these parts. Namely, lions.

When you are trekking through the bush, the high, golden grasses provide a perfect camouflage for lions. You could trip over a lion before you ever saw it. And today, we nearly did just that.

As the four of us were moving slowly across the delta, Tcori lifted his hand, signaling for us to stop. I watched curiously as he surveyed the area. It seemed like he detected something, but I couldn't be sure what. I looked around, but saw nothing out of the ordinary. Then, as if it appeared out of nowhere, a male lion rose up out of the grass just twenty feet from us.

Your instinct tells you to turn and run as fast as you can. But I knew from my research and Tcori's instructions that running from a lion is hopeless. A human can't outrun a lion, and running will only encourage an attack.

The lion was disturbed and growled ferociously. Tcori took small steps backward and signaled us to do the same. But when we followed his lead, the lion grew even more aggressive and charged. Gannon was the closest to the lion, and it went right for him. Chocs quickly lifted his rifle and took aim. I held my breath and could hardly stand to watch. Just when I expected to see the lion leap at Gannon's throat, it stopped dead in its tracks. A mock charge, just as Chocs said lions often do. But that didn't mean we were safe. The lion was still agitated and considering its options. Attack or just back away? Chocs kept his finger on the trigger, ready to fire if the lion moved any closer.

Gannon remained perfectly still. How he kept his calm in the face of what seemed like certain death is beyond me. He was actually smiling at the lion, much like a dog owner smiles at his Golden Retriever. Maybe Gannon understood that his fate was in the hands of the lion, and there wasn't a thing he could do about it. Either that, or he was scared stupid. I'm going to guess the latter. But either way, he did exactly what he was supposed to do, and it saved his life.

Tcori waved his arm, attracting the lion's attention. When the lion turned toward him, Gannon, Chocs and I slowly backed away. Tcori spoke softly in his native language, and the lion followed him. When the lion moved uncomfortably close, Tcori would swat at it with the tip of his bow. This would send the lion scampering, but he was curious and kept coming back.

Tcori's bravery was nothing short of heroic. The fact that he would risk his own life to save ours, people he hardly knew, was incredibly noble. I watched in awe as he continued to lure the lion away, until finally it lost interest and walked off, disappearing into the grass.

The male lion right before he charged - Wyatt

Botswana

Gannon
Time: Late

Well, I totally blew it! I could have gotten the most amazing lion footage ever, but when that lion popped up out of the grass, I was so scared I couldn't even lift my arms. And when he ran at me, forget it. Filming was the last thing on my mind. Anyway, having just survived the lion encounter, I felt that the worst was behind us. I mean, really? Is there anything more frightening than a charging lion? I didn't think so. But as we soon found out, there is.

❁❁❁

Part IV:

Caught in the Crosshairs of a Poacher

Gannon
Time: Who knows?

When you're trekking through the delta, it's easy to overlook the one species that is even more dangerous than a lion. The species I'm referring to is humans.

Approaching the top of a bluff, Chocs spotted a small camp hidden in the forest.

"Stay low and move quietly," he said. "We're going in for a closer look."

We crept through the bush like soldiers approaching an enemy encampment. Chocs had his rifle loaded and was ready for whatever we might encounter. I was nervous, not knowing what to expect.

When we came to the edge of the bushes, we could see the camp clearly. There was a green tarp stretched between two trees. A fire pit had been dug in the dirt. Inside the pit, embers were still smoldering. In the mud, we saw freshly pressed footprints leading out of the camp. Someone had been there not long ago.

Moving into the camp, we found a pile of elephant tusks buried under some brush. Next we came across a leopard skin hidden in the shrubs. Most gruesome of all were the bloody rhino horns that Chocs discovered in a shallow pit.

No doubt about it, this was a poacher's camp. I couldn't help but think of the poor animals that had been killed by this evil person. How someone could do that was beyond me. But my sadness quickly turned to anger. This man needed to be punished for what he had done, and it was up to us to stop him before he killed again.

We knew we didn't have much time. The poacher could return at any moment, so we worked quickly to take down his camp. Wyatt went to work with his GPS and once he had the camp's coordinates, Chocs radioed them to Jubjub, who, in turn, sent the information to the authorities. Next we took all of the tusks, skins and horns, loaded them onto a tarp and dragged them away from the camp. We purposely traveled over shrubs and grass, avoiding the sand so our footprints would be less obvious. It was hard work, and once we were about a half mile away, we hid everything under a pile of shrubs. We decided that taking these things might keep the lions safe for a while, as the poacher would probably hunt the people who had taken his possessions instead.

Just after we hid the last of the tusks, we saw a flashlight moving in the distance. We shut off our own lights and took cover but apparently not soon enough. The poacher had spotted us and immediately opened fire. There was a rapid series of explosions. It was nearly dark, but the poacher's bullets were landing close. One even splintered a tree branch right next to me. Terrified, I dove to the ground and covered my head. Bullets tore through the shrubs all around us. I thought we were goners for sure.

Chocs told us to follow him and stay low. We crawled on our stomachs through thick mud, slithering like snakes as bullets whizzed overhead. Just beyond a nearby dune, the land sloped into a dry riverbed. Once there, we were able to stand and run for safety. I've never run so fast in my life. Fortunately, the poacher did not follow.

We continued on without using our flashlights for several hours, only able to navigate by the light of a half moon. Finally, we stopped for the night under a sprawling baobab tree.

"Sorry, my friends," Chocs said, after we'd all collapsed on the ground from exhaustion. "No tents or campfire tonight. We must stay out of sight. It's likely that the poacher is tracking us. Try to get some sleep. We're moving out before sunrise."

It's safe to say that I will not sleep at all tonight. That's why I took out my journal in the first place, just to pass time. I can hardly even see what I'm writing. But other than flicking away the insects that are crawling all over me, there is not much else to do.

We are nearly out of food, and our morale is low. My stomach growls just at the thought of eating. They say the human body can survive up to six weeks without food, but I can hardly go six hours without feeling that I'm on the brink of starvation. I think I'll try to relax and focus on the sounds that echo through the bush at night. It is beautiful, the sound of Africa at night. The animals and insects create a natural symphony. So peaceful...if only we weren't being hunted by a poacher.

Wyatt
Journal Entry Date: August 30
Location: Okavango Delta, Botswana
Time: 6:08 AM
Temperature: 8 Celsius, 48 Fahrenheit
Skies: Clear
Wind: 10-15 mph, gusts to 25 mph

Today is our seventh day in the bush. I didn't expect it to take this long to find the wounded lioness and her cubs. To tell the truth, I thought we'd track them down the first day. I don't think Chocs or Tcori anticipated such a long journey either. We must, however, press on. We've been through too much to give up now.

This morning, we rationed what little food

we have left and picked some native fruits and nuts. From here on out, we will have to hunt if we want to eat anything of substance. It's important that we get some protein to improve our strength. We are growing weak.

I've taken our coordinates and calculated that we are approximately six miles southeast of the poacher's camp. We quietly radioed Jubjub again this morning, and I gave her our location. She informed us that an anti-poaching unit had been assembled and will be traveling to the delta by helicopter soon. Anti-poachers are people who hunt down and arrest poachers. We can only hope that they arrive in time.

Gannon
Date: Wyatt tells me it's day #7, I don't know
Time: Mid-morning

We are taking a short break after several hours of trekking through thick brush. Some areas were so heavy with vegetation that we had to take turns clearing a trail with a machete. We chose this path because it will be harder for the poacher to follow us.

I haven't slept in several days, and it's beginning to take its toll. I'm starting to see things that aren't really there. Twice this morning

I thought that a snake was slithering toward me, ready to strike. But each time it turned out to be nothing. It's crazy, the tricks your mind can play on you when you're tired. As my dad's friend used to say, "Exhaustion makes a coward of us all." Maintaining the courage we need to continue our mission will be a huge challenge. But we must remain positive and finish what we came to do. We absolutely must!

Wyatt
Journal Entry Date: August 30
Location: Okavango Delta, Botswana
Time: 1:21 PM
Temperature: 23 Celsius, 78 Fahrenheit
Skies: Clear
Wind: Calm

We just made an awesome discovery! Fresh lion and cub prints in the sand! Tcori said they were only hours old. The site of fresh blood droplets around the tracks makes us certain that this is the lioness we're looking for. However, the fresh blood worries me. This means that her wounds haven't clotted. The fact that she hasn't bled to death already is a miracle. We must get to her immediately!

Gannon
Journal Entry Date: The day I played with lions!
Time: Afternoon

After spotting the lion prints, we followed them through the sand into another section of forest. The ground was covered with fallen leaves and twigs, and I soon lost the trail. Apparently Tcori could see something that we couldn't because he kept moving at a fast pace.

A hundred yards or so into the forest, he turned to us and smiled. Just ahead, lying at the base of a termite mound, was the lioness and her four cubs. We didn't want to startle them, so we all took cover behind the trees. The poor lioness was lying flat on her side, panting heavily. Blood was smeared across her back hind leg. The lion cubs, unaware of their mother's grave condition, wrestled playfully in the leaves.

Tcori smeared poison on the tip of one of his arrows. He then told us to stay put, and he crept toward the lioness. One of the cubs, the runt of the litter, saw Tcori and jogged in his direction. When the lioness saw the runt running away she sprang to her feet. Her tail began to flip, and her ears went back. But she was too weak to charge. She could hardly even walk, limping on her hind leg as she moved toward Tcori. Meanwhile, the cub trotted right up to him, pawing at his leg like a cat would.

When Tcori came within about fifty feet of the lioness, he drew back the arrow and let it fly. It hit its mark, striking the lioness in the front right shoulder. She swatted it with her paw, and it fell to the ground. But the arrow had done its job, penetrating the skin and injecting the poison into her blood stream. Tcori moved the runt toward its mother with his foot. Once the cub had rejoined the others, Tcori backed off, keeping his eyes on the lioness the whole time. The lioness returned to the soft grass and fell onto her side.

"It will only be a little while before she is unconscious," Chocs said. "Once she is, we must work quickly to remove the bullet and stitch her wound. Gannon and Wyatt, your job is to occupy the cubs while we work. Remember, they may seem small and harmless, but they can give you a serious wound with their teeth and claws."

Then, like a flash, Tcori sprang to his feet and ran in the direction of the lioness.

"What's he doing?" I asked.

"Oh, no," Chocs said, pointing. "A cobra!"

Coiled up no more than ten feet from the lioness was an Egyptian cobra, one of the most venomous snakes in the whole world. Even a healthy lion would have trouble surviving a strike from one of these deadly reptiles. A weakened lion wouldn't stand a chance.

Tcori moved quickly, placing himself between the cobra and the lioness. The cobra rose up higher and fanned its hood, ready to strike. From head to tail it was probably eight-feet long! We all held our breath as Tcori faced off with this great snake. One bite would almost certainly mean death.

With the speed of a lightning strike, Tcori thrust his arm at the snake and grabbed it just under its hood. The cobra wriggled around and fought to free itself, but Tcori had a solid hold, pressing his thumb hard under the snake's jaw to prevent it from striking. Wyatt and I looked on in complete awe of Tcori's fearlessness. Truth is, a snake doesn't stand a chance against Tcori. He's way too fast.

Tcori carried the cobra far from the lioness and her cubs and set it down at the base of a bush. Luckily, the snake slithered away without putting up a fight. We all gave a huge sigh of relief. Another disaster narrowly avoided.

Wyatt
Journal Entry Date: August 30
Location: Okavango Delta, Botswana
Time: 3:27 PM
Temperature: 25 Celsius, 82 Fahrenheit
Skies: Clear
Wind: Calm

After the lioness was unconscious, Chocs and Tcori went to work on her wound. It was fun to play with the cubs, but I was more interested in the surgical procedure involved in removing the bullet. So I left Gannon in charge of what he was calling "the lion-cub daycare" and stood behind Chocs and Tcori to watch.

After sterilizing his hands with alcohol from the medical kit, Tcori dug into the wound with his fingers. He dug deeper and deeper until his hand was almost completely buried inside the lion. After some prodding, he found the bullet but couldn't get it out. It was lodged in a bone.

Then Chocs sterilized his hands, a pair of pliers and a hunting knife, and cut an incision on either side of the wound. This would give them better access to the bullet. He took the pliers and pushed them into the wound. After some maneuvering, he steadied his hand and squeezed. Sure enough, when he removed his hand from the lioness, there was a silver bullet pinched between the pliers.

Buzzing with excitement, I knelt down next to the lioness.

"You're going to be okay," I said, gently stroking the back of her head. "Everything is going to be just fine."

Suddenly, the lioness opened her eyes. My heart nearly stopped. Sitting next to an unconscious lion is one thing. Sitting next to a conscious lion is a different ballgame altogether.

Chocs and Tcori continued to stitch the wound, unaware that the lioness had woken up.

"Hey," I whispered nervously. "Better wrap it up. She's awake."

Almost as an added warning, the lioness exposed her deadly canine teeth. She hadn't eaten in days, so it seemed safe to assume that these teeth would be tearing into some poor animal's flesh in the very near future. I just wanted to make sure it wasn't my flesh.

Gannon

If you've never had the chance to play with lion cubs, you're missing out. I mean, puppies and kittens are cool and all, but a lion cub beats a dog or a cat any old day of the week.

The cubs took a liking to me right away. They all jumped up on my legs, clawing and wrestling for attention. They may be small, but, make no mistake, their teeth and claws are razor sharp. I learned this the hard way, sticking my hand in one of the cub's mouths, which was not the smartest thing to do. But the lion cubs didn't mean any harm. They just wanted to play, so that's what we did.

The runt of the litter was my favorite. He wouldn't leave my side. When I picked him up, he licked my chin so excitedly you would have thought it was covered in honey. I wanted so badly to take him home with me, but I knew that wouldn't be right. His family would miss him too much. And imagine trying to get a pet lion through airport security. Talk about a headache.

The wounded lioness with her cubs just before surgery - Gannon

Wyatt
Journal Entry Date: August 30
Location: Okavango Delta, Botswana
Time: 4:17 PM
Temperature: 23 Celsius, 78 Fahrenheit
Skies: Clear
Wind: Calm

Chocs had just sewn the last stitch when the lioness lifted her head and roared. It was good to see that her strength was returning, but it also meant that we had to get moving on the double. I tossed Chocs and Tcori their packs and dragged Gannon away from the lion cubs.

"That went as well as it could have," Chocs said, as we made fast tracks through the bush. "She will be sore for a while, but I don't believe there was any permanent damage."

I couldn't imagine that the lioness would be able to chase and kill her prey until she was back to full strength, so I asked Chocs what she would do in the meantime to feed herself and her cubs.

"She'll go after smaller animals until she is strong enough to bring down something bigger," Chocs explained. "Baby impala, warthogs, even birds. Lions are also scavengers, which means they take advantage of easy meals, like animals that die of natural causes. But I'm confident she'll be able to hunt at full strength again soon."

As we made our way back to base camp, I was on top of the world. Despite the dangers we had faced and the many obstacles we had encountered along the way, we had accomplished our mission. It was, without question, one of the proudest moments of my life. Little did we know that the greatest danger of all still lay ahead.

Moving over the grassy plains at the far end of the forest, a gunshot stopped us dead in our tracks. Before we even had time to run for cover, the poacher stepped out from behind a bush. His high-powered rifle was pointed directly at us. He wore a patch over his left eye. His right eye was black as night.

He approached us slowly. "Drop the rifle, or I'll shoot," he said. "Everyone else put your hands up."

The poacher quickly went over to Chocs, took the rifle from his shoulder and slung it over his own. Without a weapon, we had no way of defending ourselves.

"We don't want any trouble," Chocs said.

"That's too bad, mate," the poacher responded. "Because you've got some."

"Why don't we each go our own way and pretend we never saw each other?" Chocs said.

"Too late for that," the poacher said. "You

stole something of mine, and I'm here to take it back. So do yourself a favor, and tell me where I can find my tusks?"

We all stayed quiet, which only made the poacher angrier.

"Where are they?" he yelled. "I'm not going to ask again!"

Still, no one answered.

"So, you'd rather die, is that it?"

The poacher brought the rifle to his shoulder, lowered his head to the scope and took aim at Chocs.

"So be it," the poacher said.

"Wait!" I yelled. "Don't shoot! I can give you the coordinates! I wrote them down in my notebook. It's in my bag."

"Give them to me!" he said and turned his rifle on me.

I took off my backpack, set it on the ground and unzipped it. Pretending to rummage around inside the pack, I grabbed my GPS and quickly took our coordinates. I began to sweat, knowing that if the poacher discovered what I was doing, he would shoot me.

"Hurry up!" the poacher yelled. "I'm losing my patience!"

"I'm sorry," I said. "I have too much stuff in my backpack. It's almost impossible to find anything."

"Let's hope for your sake that you find it quickly!"

I knew I couldn't stall much longer. My hands were shaking like a leaf as I typed an "SOS" message into the radio and sent it to Jubjub. I could only hope that she received it.

"If you don't find it in ten seconds, I'll have you digging your own graves!"

"I found it!" I said, removing the notebook from my backpack. I opened it, turned to the page where I'd written the coordinates and tore it out.

"Here you go," I said, showing it to the poacher. "This is where you'll find your tusks, horns and skins. It's all there hidden under some brush."

The poacher yanked the paper from my hands and looked at the coordinates.

"You're obviously skilled in wilderness travel," he said. "I want you to take me there."

"I'll take you there if you let the others go," I said.

"You think you're making the rules here, do ya mate? Well, guess what, you're not!"

"If you don't let them go, you'll never find your tusks."

The poacher thought for a minute. He then gathered all of our packs and dumped them out on the ground. Sorting through our equipment, he found the radio and immediately stomped it to pieces with his heel. He also found my GPS and was about to crush it with the butt of his rifle when I stopped him.

"Don't!" I said. "We need the GPS to find our way!"

He stopped short, knelt down and picked up the GPS.

"You better not be playing games with me, boy. If I find out you are, you're finished."

"I promise, I'm not."

He put the GPS in a satchel and then searched each of us to see if we had anything hidden in our pockets.

"If you have any other radios or phones, hand them over right now. I can't have you calling the authorities."

"You've seen everything we have," Chocs said. "We have no way to communicate with the outside world."

Again, the poacher thought for a moment.

"What's to prevent you from radioing once you reach camp?"

"We're at least ten hours from our camp," I said. "I'm guessing we'll find your tusks in four hours or less. You'll have time to collect your things and go on your way long before they are able to communicate with anyone."

This information seemed to calm the poacher's nerves.

"The three of you get going!" the poacher said. He then turned to me. "Let's get moving. It will be dark before long."

"No, wait!" Chocs said, moving toward the poacher. "Take me instead!"

The poacher turned his gun on Chocs.

"Take one more step, and it will be your last."

Chocs froze.

"I'm taking the boy, and that's the last of it!"

There was nothing else Chocs could do. If he made another move, the poacher would kill him.

I nodded to Chocs to assure him that I would be okay. But to be honest, the thought of trekking through the delta at gunpoint had my stomach rumbling like an African thunderstorm. What was going to happen to me once we found the tusks, horns and leopard skin? What reason would he have for keeping me alive? This was a man who didn't have a problem with killing. He did it for a living. We had interfered with his mission, and I was sure he wanted revenge.

"Once you're there," Chocs instructed, "climb to the top of the highest tree and stay there. You'll be less vulnerable to predators and easier for us to spot. Tcori and I know the delta like the back of our hands. As soon as we arrive at camp, we'll get a vehicle and come for you."

"Enough!" the poacher yelled, pressing the barrel of his rifle in my back. "Get going and keep your hands where I can see them! Try anything and believe me, you'll regret it!"

I took what I thought might be one last look at my brother.

"If you hurt him," Gannon said, "we'll find you."

"You worry about yourself," the poacher said. "You have to cross the delta without a weapon. Chances are you'll be eaten alive before nightfall."

He turned to me. "Now, go! We have no time to waste!"

The poacher shoved me hard in the back, and we began our march. The situation seemed all but hopeless. My fate was sealed.

"Hang in there, Wyatt!" Gannon said. "We'll come for you!"

Just then I heard something in the distance. It almost sounded like a machine gun. As I turned around a helicopter suddenly rose up from behind the trees. The anti-poachers had arrived!

Gannon

When he saw the helicopter, the poacher grabbed Wyatt around the neck and put a gun to his head. The chopper landed nearby, and three men in military uniforms jumped out, all of them armed with rifles.

"Don't shoot!" I screamed. "He has my brother!"

The poacher had Wyatt in a choke hold. Wyatt fought to loosen his grip, but the poacher was much bigger and kept his arm locked tightly around Wyatt's neck.

"Come one step closer, and I'll blow this kid's head off!" the poacher yelled.

The anti-poachers stopped but kept their guns aimed at the poacher. Wyatt gasped for breath.

"Everyone put your guns down, and do it slowly!" the poacher continued.

They did as he said, laying their guns on the ground. He then motioned to the pilot to keep the helicopter running.

"Now everyone turn around and lie on the ground! I'm taking the helicopter! If anyone tries to stop me, the kid's as good as dead!"

With my legs trembling, I turned around and knelt down slowly. Just as my knee hit the dirt, a shot rang out. I spun around, horrified by what I might see. The poacher let out a scream, staggered and fell backward, gripping this thigh with both hands. Blood soaked his pants. He'd been shot in the leg.

I looked around frantically to see where the shot had come from. Jumping from the helicopter was a fourth man in camouflage. He had been hiding behind the seats and held a smoking rifle in his hands.

The other three men grabbed their rifles and ran to the poacher.

Chocs, Tcori and I ran to Wyatt as fast as we could. He was so shaken that he had fallen to the ground and could hardly breathe.

"Relax," Chocs said. "It's all over."

I helped Wyatt to his feet.

"I thought you were dead," I said.

"So did I," Wyatt said, his voice faint and unsteady.

"I knew that guy was up to no good when I saw him in Maun," I added, referring to the poacher. "I could tell by looking at him that he was evil. He had the eye of a vulture."

The men showed the poacher no sympathy as they tied his hands behind his back and dragged him across the ground to the helicopter.

The man who shot the poacher walked up and introduced himself.

"I'm General Mozello," he said. "We've

been looking for you. When we got the SOS call from Jubjub, we knew where to find you and came immediately."

"Your timing couldn't have been better," I said.

"You know, Chocs," Wyatt said, "Jubjub really is a savior."

"It seems so," Chocs said.

"That was some shot," Wyatt said. "Please tell me it wasn't just luck that you hit him and not me."

"I'm a professional sharpshooter," said the general, with a huge smile. "I can shoot a feather off an eagle from a mile away...while it's flying."

He probably wasn't joking.

"I don't know what else to say, but thank you. You saved my life."

"Glad I could be of service. A second helicopter will be arriving shortly to take you back to camp."

We watched as General Mozello's men shoved the poacher into the helicopter. He fought and squirmed to break free, but it was useless. One of the men held him down on the floor, his knees pressing into the poacher's back. As the helicopter lifted off, he stared eerily at us with his dark, sinister eye. I'm sure he was wondering how a couple of kids managed to help thwart his poaching operation, but I suppose he'll have plenty of time to figure that out in jail.

Wyatt
Journal Entry Date: August 30
Location: Okavango Delta, Botswana
Time: 8:07 PM
Temperature: 18 Celsius, 68 Fahrenheit
Skies: Clear
Wind: Calm

My parents were waiting anxiously when our helicopter landed at Shinde Camp, as was Jubjub, who ran over and hugged her dad and wouldn't let go.

"Oh, it's so good to see you boys," my mom said, tears welling up in her eyes.

"We've been worried sick," my dad said. "Mom started to think you weren't going to make it back alive."

"We thought the same thing a time or two," Gannon said.

"Or three," I added.

"I haven't been able to sleep since we received word that Wyatt was sick," my mom said. "There were no planes available in the Kalahari for several days, so we drove twelve hours on a safari bus to get here. Some of the Bushmen came with us to make sure Tcori was okay."

"Tell us what happened," my dad said. "We're dying to know."

"Wyatt fought off a croc attack," Gannon said with a smile.

I just glared at him.

"Is that true?" my mom asked.

"No," I said. "Gannon is just trying to be funny."

"Did you find the lioness?" my dad asked.

"We did," Gannon said. "And she's going to be fine."

"That's great news! What about the poacher?"

"He was shot," I said matter-of-factly.

My mom gasped and covered her mouth with her hands.

"Is he dead?" she asked in horror.

"No, but he'll probably walk with a limp the rest of his life."

"I can't believe it," my dad said, rubbing his head. "You boys really are lucky to be alive. If I'd known you were going to be in danger, I would have never let you go."

He paced back and forth.

"What kind of parents are we to send our kids into the African bush when there's a poacher in the area? I don't know what we were thinking!"

"We accomplished our mission and made it back safe," Gannon said. "That's all that matters."

"Part of me doesn't want to hear any more of your stories," my dad said, "but curiosity is going to get the best of me sooner or later. So tell us more about this adventure of yours."

"Here," I said, handing him my journal. "I've got it all documented."

"So do I," Gannon said, handing his journal to our mom.

"That's good," my mom said, "because your English grade depends on it."

For the first time in what seemed like forever, we all laughed.

"You can read them after dinner," I said. "First things first, we need something to eat."

"Yeah, what's for dinner?" Gannon asked. "We haven't had a square meal since the baboons invaded our camp and ate all our food."

"Baboons ate your food?" my dad asked. "Unbelievable! I've got to hear this."

"Read our journals."

"All right, all right. We've got some kudu steaks on the grill. They should be ready soon."

"Your sons are brave young men," Chocs said. "You should be very proud."

"We are," my mom said. "They're always up for an adventure."

"They are true explorers," Chocs said. "If Dr. Livingstone were alive today, I don't think he could find two boys better suited for an African expedition than Gannon and Wyatt."

Gannon

After dinner we met several members of Tcori's family. They had joined my parents on the safari bus and were relieved to find Tcori safe and sound. As the sky grew dark and it got colder, the Bushmen lit a campfire and celebrated with traditional songs and dances. I grabbed my camera and recorded the performance, as everyone clapped and cheered them on. My parents even joined in the dancing.

The Bushmen perform in celebration of our safe return - Gannon

We couldn't have asked for a better way to conclude our first African adventure. I say *first* for a reason. I am forever changed at having experienced this incredible place, and we've only scratched the surface. Just as so many great explorers returned to this beautiful and mysterious continent, so, too, will we.

Until next time....

Gannon and Wyatt's Travel Map

North Pole

The Alaskan Arctic

Baffin Island

Denali

Kodiak Island

Great Bear Rainforest

Cliffs of Moher, Ireland

Yellowstone Park

Stonehenge

Moab

Badlands

Niagara Falls

Paris, France

Grand Canyon

New Orleans

Barcelona, Spain

Everglades

Casablanca, Morocco

Bermuda Triangle

Tropic of Cancer

The Caribbean

Big Island, Hawaii

Galapagos Islands

The Amazon River

Machu Picchu, Peru

Tropic of Capricorn

Patagonia

Keep your eyes out for more *Travels with Gannon and Wyatt* books from some of these exciting locations!

Travels with Gannon and Wyatt

Want to become a member of the
Youth Exploration Society
just like Gannon and Wyatt?

Visit:

www.travelswithgannonandwyatt.com

That's where you'll learn how to become
a member of the *Youth Exploration Society*,
an organization of young people, like yourself,
who love to travel and are interested in
world geography, cultures and wildlife.

The website also includes:

Information about the animals in this book and
what you can do to help protect their habitat

Travel photography and video from all over the world

Information on upcoming books in the
Travels with Gannon and Wyatt series

notes

notes

notes

notes

notes

notes

Angola
Zambia
Zimbabwe
Namibia
OKAVANGO DELTA
Maun
Ghanzi
Botswana
KALAHARI DESERT
Gaborone
South Africa
Lesotho